TRANCE MISSION

by
Martin Noble
and illustrated by Joanna Roberts

HENDERSON
PUBLISHING LTD
©1996 HENDERSON PUBLISHING LTD

Chapter 1

It was him.

It was Jamie Cannon. I was sure of it.

Nobody else could dance like that – or would have dared to – like a demented chimp, waving his arms and elbows around and making silly faces.

Was he making them at me?

He was even wearing the same old baggy jeans and long-sleeved ghastly T-shirt. I couldn't make out the colours but they were probably pink, purple and ugh – a little acid-house ravy, a lot early Neanderthal bonkers. His hairstyle had changed though. He now had one of those pudding basin haircuts with hair flopping all over his eyes. What was he dancing to – heavy metal, indie or techno? Or was it still Madonna and Michael Jackson like in the old days?

Maybe he'd got stuck in a time warp.

I hadn't seen him for seven years and here we were back on opposite sides of the road again, me staring at him out of my old bedroom window, he (waving?) out of his.

He was still grinning that silly baby-faced grin just like the last time we saw each other when we were both nine. That's when my family – mum, dad, me and Sophie – who's three years my junior and Very Probably the Most Irritating Girl in the Universe – had moved with our two mangy cats from London to Swanleigh, which is in the Midlands. Jamie's family had gone off to Germany a few months later.

My name, by the way, is Abigail Edwards, which may not mean much to you, but I think I can say without false modesty that I am the only significant cultural icon in a village boasting thirty-odd houses, a pub and a single shop. A shop that doesn't even sell foaming beauty wash – which at my age, sixteen, becomes a vital weapon in warding off the effects of acne, oncoming menopausal wrinkles and senilitude.

I suppose I ought to describe what I look like, which I hate doing as most of the time I think I look completely boring. Then when I go out to a party or something, I get into a terrible state and spend ages in the bathroom staring at my reflection. Sophie says I might as well pay mum rent to live in there, which is all very well for her as she's pretty in a cute little round faced, dimple-cheeked, button-eyed, Irritating-Kid-Sister sort of way, whereas I'm just average.

I've got green eyes which are my best feature and darkish, mousy hair which I never know what to do with and most of the time it just sits around on my shoulders doing nothing in particular. If I make a special effort with the old eyeliner and make-up and I've had a decent amount of sleep I can look about six or seven on the attractive scale.

I used to be slightly small for my age until I was thirteen or fourteen when I suddenly shot up a few inches. Now I'm taller than average, which I'm pleased about, except that it makes me look even skinnier than I used to: when I get in a state about it mum says "look at all those supermodels, they're slim," and I have to remind her I am not Naomi Campbell and never will be.

"But you've got lovely eyes," mum will say; but somehow when she says it it doesn't count.

Jamie used to say he could read my eyes.

The first time he said it was a few days after he came to my primary school when he was seven.

"This is Jamie Canon," said Mrs Wyndham, our teacher.

She was a large, florid, enthusiastic woman with a posh, plummy accent, who breathed heavily all the time and wore huge flowery dresses in thick fabrics summer and winter and smelt of lilac and coal tar soap. I still remember the swishing sound her dresses made as she walked around the classroom.

"He'll be joining our class from today. Jamie's father is a famous conductor so I'm sure Jamie will have lots of things he can tell us about conducting in our music lessons, won't you, Jamie?"

He looked like a tiny little monkey in baggy short trousers that hung over his knees.

He didn't say anything but then he yawned, I now think with embarrassment, but at the time I thought, he thinks we're all boring just because his dad's a bus conductor.

"There's an empty chair next to Abigail, so go and sit next to her, Jamie."

Chrissie Somers was away that day, and she used to sit next to me. He gave me a funny stare when he sat down, as if to say, I know you don't like me but you're lumbered with me, so you'll have to put up with it and anyway it's not my fault, I didn't ask to sit next to you, did I?

We didn't talk to each other for the rest of the day, nor the next, and then it was the weekend and the following Monday Chrissie came back – she'd had the 'flu – but then she sat next to Emily Woolford and I felt very hard done by, because by then I was convinced he didn't like me and I certainly didn't like him.

The following afternoon we had art and handiwork and Mrs Wyndham handed out brand new colourful packets of modelling clay for us to model each other's faces.

I was quite pleased with mine. I'd made Jamie's look like a monkey's head.

"You've made me look like a monkey," he said.

I think it was the first time he'd spoken to me.

"That's 'cause you do look like a monkey."

"No, I don't."

"Yes, you do."

"No, I don't, and anyway, you look like a mouse."

I stared at him, offended to the core.

"That's a horrible thing to say."

"No more horrible than saying I look like a monkey. Look, there's your eyes."

He showed me the head he'd made of me and it was true. There were two little round green eyes on a blue mouse's head.

And it looked like me.

"I know what your eyes are saying," he said.

"What do you mean?"

"I can read your eyes."

"No, you can't...so what are they saying then?"

"They're saying, you wish you could sit next to Chrissie and you wish you didn't have to sit next to me."

"That's true," I said, "but then that's obvious, isn't it?"

"Hang on, I'm not finished yet, am I? And you're thinking..."

He gazed at me again in that funny way and I started to feel uncomfortable.

"*I know!*" he said suddenly, "you're thinking about ballet, aren't you?"

I stared at him.

"How did –"

"I told you, I can read your eyes. I can even see your ballet class. You enjoy doing the exercises you've learnt, but you don't like having to learn new steps. You're going to think up some excuse for not going this evening."

"But how–"

"I'm going to be a dancer when I grow up," he said. "I love dancing but not stupid old ballet. I like dancing to pop music...do you like Michael Jackson?"

"He's good, but I really like Madonna."

"She's okay. I can make myself look like a werewolf, like Michael Jackson does in the *Thriller* video. Mum tells me off though, 'cause I scare my brother. He's only four. My mum puts a blanket over the telly when *Thriller* comes on, so Mark won't be scared, but I wait 'til she goes out and take the blanket off the telly and then he starts crying, the stupid twit."

"How did you know all that about the ballet?"

"It's simple. I get these pictures in my head. No, they're not pictures, they're more like thoughts that I know don't belong to me, and I get them sometimes if I look at people's eyes. Mark can do it too. He's dead good, but he's only four so he can't describe them much... Well, actually he can't describe them at all, but I know he does 'cause...well, I just know he can. Can you do the Moonwalk? I can!"

Before I could reply, Mrs Wyndham clapped her hands to announce that we all had to place our model heads on a long table at the side of the classroom and then we would have a guessing game to see if we could identify them.

Jamie of course won.

At home that evening I couldn't stop talking about Jamie Canon who sat next to me in class and who could read people's eyes and do the Moonwalk.

I hadn't actually seen him do the Moonwalk but I just knew he would be brilliant.

A few days later Jamie came into school looking really excited.

"Guess who's moving into the house across the road from where you live?" he said.

"I give up. Who?"

"*I* am...*we* are. Mum and Dad have just bought the house. So you can come round and play and listen to my tapes and I'll show you the Moonwalk."

I was so thrilled I didn't know what to say. So I said something very stupid.

"Will your dad have his bus there?"

"Bus...what bus?"

"I thought Mrs Wyndham said your dad was a conductor."

He rolled his eyes and smirked. "Not a bus conductor. An orchestra conductor. Classical music and all that."

I felt a complete idiot, but decided to salvage some dignity out of my faux pas.

"So what does he do, just stand around waving a big stick and bowing?"

"It's better than sitting around doodling away on a drawing board, like your dad does."

My dad's a graphic designer but I hadn't told Jamie.

"How did you know that?"

"Read it in your eyes. No, actually my mum was talking to the people who live downstairs from you. I even know which is your bedroom.

It'll be opposite mine."

And it was. And Jamie did do the Moonwalk for me, which wasn't as good as Michael Jackson but nearly as good.

"Why wouldn't you do it at school?" I asked as he slid his feet up and down his bedroom floor.

He stopped and looked embarrassed.

"You'll probably think I'm stupid but I'm too shy to do it when I think anyone's watching me. It's just that when I start dancing...when I really get into it, I forget where I am and everything. My parents say I go off into a dreamworld."

"My sister's like that all the time," I said. "It's infuriating."

I told Chrissie Somers that Jamie could read my eyes. She told Emma Douglas who told Kevin Burrows and soon it was all round the class.

I didn't know about this until a few days later when someone passed me a note in class. It was torn and dog-eared and had obviously done the rounds. It read:

wotchit girls jamy canons cycic
HE CAN TELL WAT COLOUR NICKERS
YOUR WEARING

Before I could stop him Jamie had leaned across to read the note. His face went bright red and he didn't say anything for the rest of the afternoon.

I don't think he minded being teased. I often

teased him and he took it in good part, it was just that he'd told me something about him that was special and important, and it had become public property. I remember feeling that I had betrayed him, but he never once referred to it.

And he never talked about reading eyes ever again.

I still teased him about the buses though and that went on until we were nine years old.

"How's the buses?" I'd say.

"Prokofiev's well, thanks, Shostakovich is a bit under the weather."

"Who are they, ticket inspectors?"

"Anyone with half a brain would know they're composers, which rules you out."

"So what does your dad do, sing 'Any more tickets please' in E flat?"

"No he conducts – in a tuxedo."

"Why, are tuxedos lightning-resistant?"

"No, but I am." He mimicked lightning striking his head and then contorted his body as the electricity shot through it, rolling his eyes and then shot off down the road like a galvanised rabbit.

Jamie would always end an argument by running off – but then he'd always trip over and you knew he was joking. He was very good-natured – and actually very clever. Much cleverer than me.

Anyway, Jamie's father had been appointed

conductor of an orchestra in Stuttgart which is in Germany. We'd written to each other every month for the first three or four months and then a couple more times and then I'd got wrapped up in my life in Swanleigh. Swanleigh is near Stratford-on-Avon where you can now buy foaming beauty wash and see Shakespeare's plays and go to the Phoenix Pop Festival, about which more anon – and then when I was eleven I started secondary school and things got even busier and I just never got round to replying to his last letter.

I felt vaguely guilty. I remember in that letter he'd said something about his dad not being well, and something being wrong, but it was all a bit of a blur.

It was hard to see from my window, but even his funny upturned nose and freckles seemed to be the same. Chrissie Somers (who used to be my best friend and then wasn't and then was again and then wasn't and so on until I left London) used to say he was like one of those Victorian urchins you saw in postcards, pressing their noses against the windowpanes of rich people. In Jamie's case, Chrissie said, his nose just got stuck.

I was dying to go over the road and see him, but what would we say to each other? It was strange enough being back where we used to live – which was actually half of the second floor of a big Victorian house that had been divided into eight flats. The house itself looked really grand, like a hotel, but in a seedy sort of way.

My parents had kept the flat on for four years, "as our London base", they used to say (actually it was because it took that long to sell it), so we often used to come back and stay.

Mum and dad were still friends with Duncan and Nettie who'd bought the flat, and Soph had been back with them a couple of times but I'd always found some excuse not to go.

I often dreamt about the flat. In my dreams it was still my home and I was afraid it would have changed beyond all recognition.

It had of course.

"We've stripped most of the floors," Duncan said as we sat sipping preprandial cocktails in what used to be our living room but now looked more like a trendy wine bar. "It's a dirty job–"

"And the someone who has to do it is me," Nettie shouted from the kitchen.

It was gone half-past nine and we were about to eat a late supper with Duncan and Nettie but in the meantime we were just sitting around talking about art, music, politics, the cosmos and who was living in the other flats now and how much it had cost to buy the freehold. As usual Sophie didn't even bother to look interested and was listening to her Walkman.

"Oh, come on, Nettie, that's not fair. I'm either shuttling on and off the Eurostar or sitting around in some godforsaken Eastern European airport. When do I have the time?"

Duncan had something to do with imports

and exports, but I couldn't make out what.

"Well, you'd better find the time to get started on the baby's room," Nettie said pointedly as she came in with the hors d'oeuvres and patted the swelling beneath her pretty, flowered smock.

"Which room will that be?" mum asked hesitantly – I could tell she was feeling *un peu* wistful, like me, even though she'd had time to absorb the changes.

"The little front room–" Duncan started to say.

"My bedroom," I blurted out, and then blushed. "I'm sorry, I mean–"

"It's all right, Abi," Nettie said gently. "I know you felt a bit nervous about coming back here, but you know you're always welcome to come and stay, any time – you could even come on your own if you want, if that's all right with you, Paul and Fiona?"

My parents nodded happily (which I thought was a bit two-faced of them because they're always moaning on at me about not wanting to do things with them as a family any more, but they'll grow out of it). Fortunately Soph was plugged into her headphones, otherwise she would have been bound to say "What about me?".

"Anyway," Nettie went on, "for the time being, the room's more or less as you left it, fortunately for you. Actually, there are still quite a few loose floorboards – we'll have to replace them." She glared at Duncan.

"Maybe I can get a start-up loan from the

EC," he said, and then began wittering on about the single European currency.

I was getting extremely bored extremely quickly. I muttered an excuse and left Sophie to her groany old compilation of last year's chart hits and went for a wander around the flat.

Everything had changed: instead of the old threadbare Indian carpets there were stripped varnished floorboards with tasteful rugs, huge Mexican cheese plants, Japanese screens and Italian prints on the walls, which had been repainted in muted colours with names like Mellow Seahaze and Autumn Dreamscape.

It looked much more elegant than when we lived there. I liked what they'd done but it somehow seemed wrong, as if you'd gone to a party with all your friends and your parents had turned up looking all young and trendy.

I felt sad and a bit shocked. Another bit of my childhood had slipped away.

I had reached the end of the corridor that led back to the front door. My bedroom was on the right.

Nervously I pushed the door open, very slightly.

There was a gentle creaking sound which I knew like an old friend. Slightly relieved I closed my eyes tightly, pushed the door open, held my breath and switched on the light. Then I opened my eyes.

The room was in near darkness. I squeezed

myself through two aisles of cardboard boxes and as my eyes began to adjust I could see the empty light bulb fitting hanging forlornly from the ceiling. Nettie was nearly right – the room was "more or less" as I'd left it. There were boxes everywhere, rolls of wallpaper and stacks of framed paintings, towers of hi-fi, chairs and a table.

They had done nothing radical at all apart from turn it into a junkroom.

"Heigh-ho," I sighed to myself, and then, looking more closely, I started to recognise a few familiar landmarks: my old bed and some bits of furniture I'd left behind, like the wooden trolley I kept my books and games on. We used to call it the 'Benny Binder' after an old friend of my great-aunt who'd been given it as a wedding present. It was falling to pieces when my parents put it in my room. Dad was always meaning to fix it, but never got round to it. A bit like Benny Binder himself probably. I was glad it was still there.

In the corner, wedged between the fireplace and the wardrobe, I found some abandoned toys: a few dried-up felt-tip pens, a notice board studded with badges, a jar of beads, a red plastic castle, a couple of Sindy dolls, some combs and a hairbrush. I picked up the hairbrush and absently started to brush Sindy's hair, and then remembered I was sixteen.

Outside, in the main road that led into the South Circular Road, the streetlamps had come on. I peered out of the window at the continuous flow of traffic, so different from Swanleigh with its thirty-odd houses, pub and single shop. I remembered that the traffic was always so bad that mum and dad would make Sophie hold my hand just to cross the road to Jamie's house. Sometimes mum or dad or Fran, Jamie's mother, would drive us all – me, Sophie, Jamie and his brother Mark – up the hill to school, but more often we walked.

I gazed at the rambling Edwardian house on the corner opposite where Jamie used to live. There was something different about that house too, but it wasn't anything obvious, no yuppie facelifts there. If anything it seemed not so much unlived in as dead...or in a trance...I shivered and hugged myself even though the evening was warm and humid. The windows looked black and vacant like the man with no eyes...

The thought made me shudder. A few months before, I'd spent the day with my friend Lizzie Hubble in Oxford. Lizzie has sickeningly perfect skin and blonde hair and everything else that boys go for, but she's a really good friend with a wicked sense of humour.

Anyway, we found ourselves wandering the back streets, not really sure where we were. We'd turned a corner and come face to face with a man whose eyes were missing from their sockets. I'd hardly had time to register the fact when he smiled at me.

I felt awful, guilty that I was so shocked: yet

upset as though he'd deliberately set out to shock me. I know that sounds mad. I've often seen blind people, with or without dark glasses, yet this was different. I still thought of that man, those eyeless sockets, and tried hard to remember that he was still a human being.

It was getting darker. I turned and looked around the room, wondering whether my bedroom window had the same vacant, uninhabited look.

It was when I turned back that I saw Jamie, dancing in the window.

They were talking about Third World famine and civil war when I got back to the living room.

"Where've you been?" said Sophie indignantly. "We've been waiting for ages to eat and I'm dying of starvation thanks to you."

The nearest Sophie ever got to dying of famine and starvation was when she ran out of chocolate, but the smell of Nettie's lasagne and talk of starving millions had obviously got the better of forty totally boring smash hits.

I gave her one of my withering looks. "I'll come and visit you in the anorexia ward. Mum, do you mind if I just pop over the road – I think I've just seen Jamie Canon."

"But Abi, we're about to eat."

"I won't be long, I promise."

"Can I go too?" Sophie piped in predictably.

"No!" mum and I said together.

"If she can go, why can't *I*?"

"We didn't say either of you could go," mum

18

said, and looked across at dad for moral support.

"But Mum–"

"Fi, let her go," dad said. "I'm sure Duncan and Nettie won't mind, will you?"

They shook their heads vehemently and I smiled gratefully at dad. "Well, Okay then, but don't be long," mum smiled.

"What about me? I want to see Mark," said Sophie, glowering.

"Hard luck, he's not at home. Anyway, you don't even remember him."

"Of course I do. We started school together. He was my first boy–" She stopped and blushed.

I couldn't resist it.

"At last Sophie Edwards reveals all in tomorrow's tabloids. 'Mark Canon was my first and only love–'"

"Oh shut up, you pain."

"Come on, you two," said dad. "Look, Abi, you can go and see Jamie on the condition you take Soph with you."

Sophie looked revoltingly smug.

For a moment I considered decapitating her but decided it would be too messy.

"Come on, then," I said, making for the door, "but for goodness' sake, don't embarrass me."

"Me embarrass you!" she said, following me out noisily.

Chapter 2

Outside it was already dusk. Instinctively I took Sophie's hand to cross the road and instinctively she took mine...and then pushed me away. But as we got to the gate I felt Sophie shiver and reach for my hand again. I held hers gratefully.

I registered with mild curiosity that it was a new gate: not the rusty old cast iron gate I remembered, but a bigger, more solid-looking one. At the same time I noticed the high walls surrounding the garden.

Then I realised that the walls were camouflaged by a thick mass of ivy that blended with the greenery of the garden and that was why I hadn't spotted them earlier. The gate was actually quite elaborate, so that although it looked from a distance like a normal gate, painted an unobtrusive green, it was actually constructed of thick steel and was firmly locked, with an Entryphone buzzer system to one side.

I pressed the buzzer and we waited. The house seemed even more forbidding than it had looked from my window.

It suddenly occurred to me that the house was once again plunged into darkness with no sign of life from any of the windows.

How was that possible? Surely I hadn't imagined seeing Jamie. Could he possibly have left the house in the short time it had taken to come across the road? He couldn't have gone to bed – it was barely ten o'clock.

There was a noise on the Entryphone and then a female voice.

"Yes?"

"I'm Abi...I came to see Jamie."

There was a long pause and then the voice came back.

"Please wait."

A buzzer sounded and the gate opened: I looked at Sophie and she shrugged back at me and we walked up to the front door. There was no doorbell so we just stood there waiting.

There was an eerie silence and then we both heard the sound of a dog barking. It seemed to be coming from deep within the house and after a minute it stopped.

"I don't like this at all," Sophie whispered. "I thought you said you'd seen Jamie." Sophie shivered. "I don't like this at all," she repeated. "It's creepy."

"I did see him. He was at the window, dancing. I think he waved to me. You'll see him in a minute. And darling Marky no doubt."

I tried tapping on the door and this time the barking was even louder.

Sophie's hand tightened on mine. "Let's go," she said. "I don't know why we came. Anyway, I'm starving."

"I didn't ask you to come but now you're here I'm not letting you go back on your own."

To tell the truth I was grateful that Sophie was with me, and anyway, before this turned into a full-scale argument, the barking grew even louder. I remembered Jonah, the Canons' Jack Russell, that used to yap nearly as irritatingly as Sophie, but this wasn't Jonah. It sounded more like an Alsatian.

"Shhhh," I whispered, anticipating some inanity from Soph. Beneath the barking I could hear muffled voices, then a door slammed shut. After a brief pause came the sound of footsteps and the front door opened.

I was right. Big Bad Jonah was a huge Alsatian, baring its teeth and growling at us. Fortunately it was on a lead. Unfortunately its owner wasn't and she looked even more fierce.

"Can I help you?"

This woman was certainly not Jamie's mum Frances.

Mrs Munster, Soph and I later agreed, had somehow escaped from Hollywood and taken up residence in Jamie's house: at least six inches taller than Frances, dressed as though for a business meeting, in a well-tailored black twin-set. Her black hair, greying slightly at the temples, was immaculately swept back to reveal a face that would send young children screaming for their mothers.

"I...we came to see Jamie," I stuttered.

She stared at us, particularly at me.

"I think you are mistaken. There is no such person here."

Her voice was deep, cold, with maybe an accent, but I was too bewildered to wonder about that.

"But...I saw him, just now...at the window."

She stared at me again and frowned. "That is not possible."

Big Bad Jonah seemed to agree and growled even more menacingly.

"But I did!"

I felt myself growing hot with anger. I tried to look past her but the hallway was dark and I could hear nothing apart from the dog's growling.

"Come on, Abi, let's go," Sophie hissed.

I know it was childish but I felt like crying. "I want to see Jamie now!" I found myself saying in a high, shrill voice.

"Please wait there."

To my surprise she slammed the door shut, perhaps worried that we'd follow her into the house.

"Please, Abigail, can we just go?" Sophie pleaded. I could tell she was as upset as I was because she used my full name, but I wasn't in any mood to tease her.

"Look, Soph, go if you want. I'll be back soon, I promise."

She opened her mouth to speak, but she could see I was determined to stay.

"You're always doing this," she muttered. "You're a fascist."

"Fascist? Moi?"

"Yes, like Hitler and Mussoloni or whatever his name was. And Margaret Thatcher."

"You're too young to remember Margaret Thatcher," I said.

"No I'm not, and you're just like her."

"Okay. So why am I like Margaret Thatcher?"

"Because she said, 'You turn. This lady's not for turning.' And that's you. That's what you said."

"Which quiz show did you pick that titbit up from – or was it Trivial Pursuit?"

"I don't spend all my time watching telly like some people," Sophie said.

"No, you spend all your time listening to dumb chart music."

"At least it's performed by living human beings and not machines. Or boring old drones who just stand there like zombies with big eyebrows."

Sophie's knowledge of decent techno and indie was somewhat hampered by the fact that she was clinically brain dead.

"What do you know about it anyway? You're musically challenged, i.e. tone deaf. You only go for the looks."

Our uplifting badinage was interrupted by the door opening again. This time, to my blessed relief, the dog was nowhere to be seen or heard and instead of Mrs Munster, we were greeted by a man who was the spitting image of the actor who played Dr Doolittle in the film. Maybe he'd had a friendly chat with Big Bad Jonah and the Alsatian had agreed to call it quits. He looked like he'd spent a long time in the sun or under a UV lamp. He must have been at least in his fifties with lines etched in his forehead and big bags under piercing blue eyes, and long flowing greyish hair to make up for his receding hairline.

I couldn't take my eyes off him.

"I understand you're under the impression that someone called Jamie lives here," he said in a smooth, velvety voice that made my skin crawl.

"He did live here, seven years ago, and...and I saw him here tonight, in the window."

Dr Doolittle smiled. "I'm really sorry, er..."

"Abigail."

"I'm sorry, Abigail, but this is not possible. What was his surname?"

"Canon...Jamie Canon."

"Ah yes, the Canons. We bought the freehold of this property from the Canons' estate. I negotiated for the property while I was in Germany. So I accept that this...Jamie Canon, did live here but now..." he smiled again, "as you see...no."

"Estate?" I asked faintly. "Do you mean–"

He nodded sadly. "I can see this may have come as a shock to you, but I understand from the Canons' solicitors that the whole family – all four of them – were killed in a car crash some years ago."

"But I saw him in the window upstairs. From my window, there." I pointed to my bedroom window across the road, which was also now shrouded in blackness.

Did I imagine it? Far back in the house, almost it seemed, *under* the house, I thought I heard a muffled cry.

He paused and something in his face seemed to change. Have you ever watched someone driving and coming to a dangerous bend? You could actually see him almost deciding to switch on his concentration, to go into a different gear.

"Impossible," he said slowly and rhythmically, almost like a chant. "Perhaps the lamplight and the leaves, the shadows, made you imagine–"

As he spoke, his blue eyes seemed to be drilling into me, and for a few seconds I thought I was going to pass out. I felt myself reeling and was finding it hard to breathe. His words seemed to amplify and echo in my mind, like the repeated sampling and reverb you get in techno.

"Impossible ... impossible ... lamplight ... lamplight ... leaves ... leaves ... shadows ... shadows ... imagine ... imagine ... imagine ... imagine–"

With a huge effort I pulled myself together and glanced at Sophie. Her eyes were drooping and her hand was now limp in mine.

"I didn't imagine it..."

He sighed. "I'm sorry, I must go now."

He bowed and closed the door.

As soon as he had gone we both seemed to snap out of whatever it was we had snapped into, though I was too upset to say anything as we walked back to the old house. As we climbed the stairs to the second floor, Sophie came to a halt.

"Did you see what I saw?"

"What?"

"In their garden, in the tree. It looked like one of those, what do you call them, survelance cameras."

"Surveillance."

"Yup. In the tree. I wonder what they've got to protect."

I suddenly remembered the muffled cry.

"Maybe it's like Colditz," I said.

"What's that?"

"It was a German prisoner of war camp. Maybe it's not so much who they don't want to let in, as who they don't want to let out."

Chapter 3

"So either you imagined you saw Jamie," said dad as we sat round Duncan and Nettie's table, and I'd wiped my tears and ate what I could of the lasagne, "or you did see him–"

"In which case he didn't die in a car crash," I said.

"...but they don't know he's gone back there," dad went on sceptically.

"Or they do know he's there and they're lying," I said.

"Well, they're an odd couple, the Polsons, but I doubt whether they're criminal types," Duncan said. "Moved in at the beginning of the year. Keep to themselves. I parked my Volvo a little too close to his driveway once at the back so he couldn't get his car out, but he was quite civil. Distant though. Didn't really want to chat."

I remembered the back driveway. The Canons' house was on the corner of Somerset Road – the main road where we used to live – and Farley Rise which led up to the school. A fence surrounded the property and at the end of this was a large gate which was the Canons' driveway. At the back of the driveway there used to be a broken fence. For a few months, when we were seven or eight, Jamie and I had crawled through this fence and made a hidey hole for ourselves.

"And you've never seen the Canon kids?"

dad asked.

"No. Mind you, I haven't really been looking for them. What about you, Net?"

"Sorry, no." She looked at me sympathetically as if to say, sorry to let you down. I smiled and shrugged.

"All I've noticed," she continued, "is that they always go out every Wednesday between three and six in the afternoon, regular as clockwork."

"Perhaps they go to church," said Sophie cynically.

"The Hellfire Club coven meeting more likely," I muttered.

"There's always a fourth alternative," said mum.

We all looked at her and I knew what was coming. Mum was into lots of New Age type stuff, tarot and meditation and palmistry. We used to laugh at her but at least she didn't spend all her time going to Tupperware parties or coffee mornings to prattle on about babies and flower arranging, like some of the other women in our village.

"What you saw was a ghost."

"No, it couldn't have been," I said confidently, but even as I said it I could feel the doubts creeping in. "I don't believe that. He was so real, just like he used to be."

"There's more than one type of ghost," mum said. "For instance, it could have been the ghost of Jamie as you remember him seven years ago, a kind of electrical imprint–"

"No."

"Or possibly it could be a projection coming from you."

"Which is another way of saying I imagined it."

"Not exactly. The mind is very powerful – it's possible that you're a kind of medium through which Jamie can continue his existence."

I shook my head. "No. I can't accept that."

"Then again, Jamie's actual entity – Jamie himself, his living spirit – may have returned to the house."

"I'm sorry, it's just not–" I felt myself starting to cry again.

"I'm sorry, Abi, I didn't mean to upset you," mum said gently. "We don't know what the truth is, none of us. But there has to be an explanation."

"Well, I don't believe in ghosts," said Duncan. For a moment I felt grateful to have him as an ally but then he added, "You probably just imagined the whole thing."

Nettie darted him an angry look.

"Polson said they were all killed in the car crash?" dad asked.

"He said 'all four'..." Sophie began. We stared at each other. "Which means that–"

"One of them at least is still alive!" I said.

Duncan and Nettie looked puzzled.

"There were three children," mum explained. "They had an older daughter called Natalie. As far as we know she went with them to Stuttgart. So one of the Canons wasn't in the car."

"If there really was a car crash," I muttered.

"Well, maybe I can help out there," said Duncan. "I'm off to Germany next week. I'll see what I can rake up."

"Oh, would you?" I said, warming to him again.

"Can't promise too much. The police can be stroppy about enquiries from the general public, especially non-natives, but I know a chap on *Der Spiegel*. Anyway I'll do my best."

Back at school in Swanleigh my exams were about to begin. For the first few days I kept seeing Jamie dancing in the window – the image popping up in my head like a gremlin in a computer game, but exams soon distracted me, and so did Thomas who had sort of been my boyfriend except that we broke up the night before my French oral. I wasn't really upset about this: I'd been thinking of dumping him for some time. I occasionally enjoy watching sci-fi videos and playing computer games but you can't spend twenty-four hours a day on them, which was what Thomas did. He's quite good-looking in a pale, interesting sort of way, but after the initial attraction I realised I didn't really fancy him, and in any case we just didn't like the same music, so I felt relieved that he was the one who dumped me.

I know this may sound callous but the thing

that upset me most was that just before we broke up I'd managed to get my parents to pay for two tickets for the Phoenix Pop Festival and I'd already given Thomas his ticket.

So I got my friend Lizzie – she of the sickeningly perfect skin and blonde hair and everything else that boys go for – to chat Thomas up and persuade him to let her have the ticket. If he was expecting a night of unbridled passion with her he was in for a cruel disappointment, because Lizzie only goes for boys who are even more perfect than she is and they had so far proved unobtainable.

As it turned out she did agree to go to a Star Trek convention with Thomas – and met some really gorgeous boy there, by which time Thomas had got over her and got off with some Trekkie, so in the end everyone got what they wanted.

The day we went to the Phoenix was gloriously sunny: the kind of day you never wanted to end though you knew it would, apart from the queues for the ladies' lavatories which you thought would never end, which in fact was true. We managed to see all the bands we both wanted to see, snack at various exotic food tents, and avoid spending whatever money we had left on all the ethnic and New Age stuff you get at festivals.

Then we decided to try the Megadog dance tent.

Personally I'm not into the kind of raves where drugs are taken. I've never taken any drugs myself but I've known kids, not only older but also younger than me, who've taken them and in one or two cases it has really screwed them up.

As far as I'm concerned you can get high and enjoy yourself without having to mess up your system in the process. I know many kids who enjoy raves without needing to take ecstasy and I was looking forward to dancing to techno, which I love.

I wasn't disappointed. Lizzie and I were soon really into the music which veered from slow and dreamy ambient and trance to frenetic techno and jungle.

At first I wasn't aware of him. He was just a boy dancing wildly somewhere in the corner of my vision.

And then I recognised him.

It was Jamie.

He looked just the same as he had when I had seen him through the window of his house across the road, happy, animated, and yet still seeming to be in a world of his own, unaware of anyone around him.

I tugged at Lizzie but she was in her own little Hubble bubble.

"It's him, Lizzie," I shouted to make myself heard above the music.

"What!"

"Jamie, the one I told you about. The boy I used to know in London who I saw again last time I was there."

"Where?"

I pointed to where Jamie was still dancing, though now he was half-hidden by other dancers.

"Which one?" she shouted.

"In the psychedelic orange T-shirt."

She nodded, spotting him. "He looks sweet. Why don't you go and talk to him?"

"What do I say?"

"Tell him who you are. Find out if it's him."

Something made me hesitate. Perhaps it was because he had looked so happy, so self-contained, that I didn't want to break into his little haven of contentment. Maybe I suddenly felt a little shy. Whatever, by the time I had made up my mind to follow her advice, Jamie had disappeared.

I tried to find him but the dance area was poorly lit and he seemed to have just been swallowed up in the crowd.

Had it really been him? Was I imagining it again? I had so many questions in my mind and I couldn't seem to think straight.

By the time I found Lizzie again I had given up searching for him.

There was a strange expression on her face but I could hardly register what she was saying and she had to drag me out of the dance tent before we could talk.

"He's a real weirdo, your friend," she said.

"What do you mean?"

"I saw him leaving the tent. He looked like a zombie, like someone had pulled the plug out on him."

At least, whoever it was, Lizzie had seen him too, but this was small comfort.

"Maybe he was still into the music," I said glumly.

Lizzie stared at me and shook her head. "No, this wasn't trance. It was more like...death."

Chapter 4

Duncan had yet to come up with anything in his enquiries about what might have happened to the Canons in Germany. After the Phoenix Festival, as the summer holidays stretched ahead, I had a curious sense of anticlimax as though I had found something very precious and lost it again.

For the first two weeks I went camping in Brittany with my family, but unlike previous years I felt homesick and couldn't wait to be back in Swanleigh. When we got back, Lizzie rang me to tell me she had tickets for the Reading Festival at the end of the month and my first thought, though I know it was totally silly, was that maybe I would see Jamie again.

My exam results came through in the third week of August. They were decent enough – one A (for English), five Bs and a couple of Cs – and as I'd already bribed mum and dad into giving me a cash bonus on top of my pocket money I had enough cash now to spend on some decent new gear for the Reading Festival.

Of course Sophie had also wanted to go, which would have ruined everything, but my parents came to the rescue by saying she could go next year.

As the Reading Festival approached I had a stupid sense of excitement that was somehow wrapped up with the possibility of seeing

Jamie again.

I know it didn't make sense. It had been pure chance that I had seen him in the Megadog tent at the Phoenix and the chances of seeing him again at Reading were smaller than winning the jackpot in the National Lottery.

But something seemed to have changed inside me. It was as though since the first time I had seen Jamie again in London I had slipped into another dimension, a kind of dream world in which I somehow knew that I had to see him again.

One night in France I had even dreamt that we were back in my old flat, playing hide and seek. It was my turn to search for him and I heard him calling me from my room.

"I'm here, Abi. I bet you can't find me!"

I looked around the room but he was nowhere to be seen.

"I'm down here, Abi."

I looked down and noticed a crack in the floorboards directly underneath me which grew bigger and bigger. As I tried desperately to step out of the way, I stumbled and fell into the gap.

I screamed but I couldn't be heard as I descended into the blackness...

I still remembered the terror I felt on waking up. And yet I felt Jamie was still there in my waking life, calling me to find him.

And then Polson's voice would reverberate hypnotically in my mind:

Impossible...impossible...lamplight...

lamplight...leaves...leaves...shadows... shadows
...imagine...imagine...imagine...imagine...

The Reading Festival was, for Lizzie and me, on a much grander scale than the Phoenix because we were to be there for three days, camping out. Mum and dad had grumbled a bit that I was too young to be there on my own at a pop festival for three days. I'd told them I'd be perfectly Okay, and anyway I'd be with Lizzie. Lizzie's parents didn't have a problem with it so why did mum and dad? Anyway, they gave in, and then Lizzie told me that her parents had said the same thing and she'd given the same reply as I had.

Almost as soon as we arrived I realised just how ridiculous I had been assuming I was going to bump into Jamie. Though I would sometimes find myself looking around the crowds for a fluorescent orange T-shirt, there were too many distractions, such as Robbie Connors.

Robbie was a year older than me, in the sixth-form college at Swanleigh where I would be starting in September, and normally he would never have noticed me, let alone have spoken to me.

Reading seemed to break down those barriers and I was starting to wonder why I had spent so much time thinking about someone who was mainly just a memory from my childhood, and whose present existence could well have been a figment of my imagination.

Maybe Polson had been speaking the truth and Jamie had died in the car crash.

After I'd stopped seeing Thomas I had been in no hurry to get another boyfriend. I know some girls who can't seem to function without one, but I think friends – real friends, male or female – are more important, and I would rather wait for the 'real thing'. I'm not sure whether that makes me a hopeless romantic or hopelessly unromantic, and frankly I don't really care.

Anyway, during the first two days at Reading, Robbie and I became good friends – and I do mean just friends, especially after he confessed to me that he fancied Sarah Matthews, who's also in sixth-form college and whose sister Jackie is in my class. Sarah and Jackie were there at Reading and so I worked with Robbie on a campaign to get her to go out with him.

Unfortunately it worked out brilliantly, so by Sunday, the last day of Reading, I was back with Lizzie, who by this time had broken her golden rule and had found herself a long-haired hippie who was at least two years older than her and was only too obtainable. As the morning wore on I began to feel more and more like a gooseberry and decided to go off on my own.

Unlike the Phoenix which had all types of music, the Reading Festival has more rock and indie-type music and there were no dance tents for me to wander into. I had noticed a dance club, which would mean forking out more money, and had not given it much thought, but now, without Lizzie or Robbie around, I found myself once again thinking of Jamie.

I'm here, Abi, I bet you can't find me.

With a sense of being wasteful and irresponsible, I paid my money and entered the club. At first it was difficult to make out anyone's features in the swirl of dancers, the flashing of strobe lights. On the far wall continuously changing psychedelic images were projected onto a huge screen, while techno and Goa trance were pumping out of the 10K speakers at deafening decibel levels. The combined sweat of the dancers drenched the atmosphere.

Feeling very self-conscious standing there on my own, I began hesitantly to dance, but after only a few minutes I started to lose myself in the music.

I closed my eyes and seemed to see Jamie dancing in front of me, holding out his hand to me and grinning. The vision seemed so real that I finally had to open my eyes again.

I felt as though I had touched a live two hundred and forty volt wire.

He was dancing in front of me. A happy, contented smile lit up his face, but once again I couldn't tell whether he was smiling at me.

This time I had to know.

40

I reached over and touched his face. For a moment he seemed startled, then he laughed and carried on dancing.

I felt really foolish. Suppose it wasn't Jamie? What could I say to him now? I continued dancing, determined this time not to let him out of my sight. Occasionally he would turn and dance a few feet away from me, and once or twice another dancer interposed themselves between us and I would edge myself back into place as near to him as I could.

For some reason I was still too shy to speak to him.

My energy was starting to flag and I was wondering just how long he would carry on dancing, when he suddenly turned and began to make for the exit.

I followed hard on his heels, pushing my way through the dancers, knowing that if I lost him this time I would never forgive myself. We were just a few feet apart as I rushed up the steps that led to the exit door, when he stopped and turned.

There was a frown on his face.

"Are you following me?"

"No!...I mean...yes!" I stammered.

He grinned. "I didn't know I had such pulling power!... Who are you?"

I stared at him uncertainly.

"My name's Abigail Edwards," I said slowly, searching his eyes for some sign of recognition.

There was none.

"Hi, Abigail Edwards, pleased to meet you."

"Is your name...Jamie Canon?"

For a second I could swear he looked disconcerted, but then the serenity I had seen earlier returned to his face and I thought maybe I had imagined it.

"That's a funny name. Sounds like a cowboy ...or a photocopier."

My heart sank.

"It's the name of a boy I used to know in London," I said, feeling totally stupid and embarrassed. "We used to go to the same school and he lived opposite me. I haven't seen him for years, but then I thought I saw him in his old house and...he looked just like you... And he danced like you."

"Poor chap. I thought I was the only one. Maybe we should meet and swap a few dance steps... Sorry," he added when he saw the look on my face, "I didn't mean to sound flippant."

"Well, you did," I muttered.

For a moment neither of us seemed to know what to say.

"Look, I meant what I said," he jumped in. "I really am pleased to meet you. I don't know anyone here."

"So...what's your name?" I asked, a little mollified.

He grinned again and then did a somersault.

"What kind of answer is that?" I said, amused and exasperated at the same time.

In reply, he turned on his heels and ran off

so that I had to sprint for five minutes to catch up with him. He suddenly tripped over a few yards in front of me and in turn I tripped over him, so that we collapsed on top of each other in hysterics on the grass.

When we had recovered I gazed at him. It was just the kind of thing Jamie would have done.

"Are you sure you're not Jamie Canon?" I asked.

"Are you sure you are Abigail Edwards?"

I sighed. "Then who are you?"

He faltered and then gave me an odd look, as though trying to remember something.

"I'm...a transmitter."

I thought I hadn't heard him right.

"You're a what?"

"A transmitter," he repeated almost tonelessly.

"I don't know what you mean."

"Transmission...trance mission."

His face had gone all dreamy as if he were in a trance. Then he looked confused as if he didn't understand what he had said either.

"What on earth does that mean?"

He grinned. "God knows – maybe you've got the key."

"Well, Jamie's dad, Richard, was a conductor... you don't mean that, do you? Do you conduct?"

I know it was a silly question, but I was desperate for some sign of recognition, even just a flicker, and maybe I imagined it but for a few moments a dreamy, faraway look came into his eyes.

I suddenly remembered the expression on his face as he was dancing in the club, as if he were on another planet. "You're not...have you taken something?" I asked cautiously.

It was his turn to look perplexed. "What do you mean?"

"I suppose I mean drugs – dope, ecstasy, I don't know. Do you take them?"

He looked disgusted. "Of course not. What gave you that idea?"

"You seem so...you look so happy, and yet a bit lost at the same time."

I could see him thinking about this. "Well, I am very happy, here, now, with you. So if I am lost I suppose I don't want to be found."

"And you're not on drugs?"

He stood up and pulled me up with him. "Look, I really don't know anything about drugs and I certainly haven't taken any. All I know is that I've always liked dancing to this kind of music and when I'm dancing I seem to get right out of my head. I can forget the bad things."

"What bad things?"

He shrugged. "Oh, you know...don't you sometimes want to forget who you are and just ...enjoy being."

I thought about this. "No, I can't say I've ever wanted to forget who I am. Except maybe when I'm with Sophie – she's my kid sister – and she says something totally, excruciatingly embarrassing and I just want to disappear into the ground."

His eyes lit up as though he had remembered something. "That's where I come from."

"Where?"

"Somewhere down there." He pointed downwards to the earth...

He still wouldn't tell me his name or where he really came from and everything he said seemed to have an odd sort of double meaning, but I didn't think he was trying to be mysterious: I think he was genuinely replying to my questions the only way he could. And although he had said he wasn't Jamie, in some part of my mind I still believed he was.

"Okay then, if you won't tell me your name," I said as we made our way towards one of the main stages, "what do I call you?"

He thought for a moment as though he himself accepted that telling me his name was out of bounds.

"Well, as we met dancing to trance, why not call me Trancer?"

"Trancer?"

"Yes?" he replied, already having taken on the name.

We both laughed and after that we spent the rest of the afternoon together. I decided that whoever he was, I liked him.

The time seemed to fly by with him: we watched bands, drove on the dodgems at the funfair, and never stopped talking to each other.

I couldn't tell you what we said, though,

because it would sound like nonsense. I still knew nothing about him, but I knew the important things – his quirky sense of fun and his bright intelligence.

Towards the end of the afternoon I thought I detected a few moments when he grew tense and as dusk approached we fell quiet. At first it was what is known as a companionable silence but then, suddenly, it wasn't. Within minutes, he seemed to grow sullen and I felt that if I had tried to say anything he wouldn't have replied. I could see his face becoming drawn, and then expressionless.

"Trancer?" I said anxiously, "Are you all right?"

He stared ahead ignoring me.

I remembered what Lizzie had said.

He looked like a zombie, like someone had pulled the plug out on him... This wasn't trance. It was more like...death.

I felt a cold shiver of horror as the truth dawned on me. Trancer was changing in front of my eyes into the lifeless zombie Lizzie had seen leaving the Megadog dance tent.

"Trancer?"

He slowly turned his head towards me.

His eyes had grown vacant like the blindman we had seen in Oxford earlier in the year.

Suddenly there was a loud shriek of laughter from a group of people behind us and I turned to see what the commotion was.

When I looked back, Trancer had vanished.

Chapter 5

I spent most of my last evening at the Reading Festival searching for Trancer, though I felt instinctively that the search was hopeless. Even if I had found him I wouldn't have known what to say to him, and I dreaded seeing him again in that way – like a body without a mind.

Whoever he had turned into I was sure it wasn't the effect of drugs. In the few hours we had spent together I had developed a special link of trust and friendship with him.

And I was convinced that whatever had drained him of his presence and energy was in some way connected with 'the bad things' in his life. The things he came to the festival to get away from. Could he himself remember what they were? I doubted it. I felt he must be leading a double life, and I suspected that each of those lives knew little about the other one.

But this was all guesswork. Trancer had disappeared again and I had no way of getting back in touch with him. Even now I still sensed that he and Jamie were the same person, but how could I prove it?

Back at home the phrase Trancer had used kept returning to me:

I'm a transmitter...transmission...trance mission.

Why did he say this and what did it mean? I thought about transmitters and decided to look up the word in my encyclopaedia. This is what it said:

'**transmitter** (communications), in telephony refers to the carbon microphone or transducer that picks up sound waves and converts them into electrical signals. In radio, it refers to the equipment for generating and broadcasting radio signals that form a part of the communications link.'

Physics isn't one of my strong subjects, I prefer Art and English and French, which were the subjects I would be taking later on, so I really had to puzzle over this definition before I gave in and decided to ask my parents. Dad's good at explaining scientific stuff but that didn't really explain how a human being could be a transmitter.

It was actually mum who seemed to understand.

"I suppose what you're asking, Abi, is how can a person generate and then transmit signals like a radio transmitter does – and nobody really knows the answer.

"After all, science doesn't even recognise that people can do it. But the real mystery is that it does happen. There's enough evidence to show that the brain itself transmits, not just through the five senses of our body so that we can speak and move and act, but that people transmit their thoughts to others without physical speech–"

"You mean telepathy."

"Exactly."

"So is that what Trancer meant when he said he was a transmitter – that he could transmit thoughts to other people?"

"Well, I don't know–"

"Come on, Fiona," dad sighed sceptically, "you don't know. No one does, and I don't think you should be putting those ideas into Abi's head."

"You mean Mum's practising telepathy?" Sophie chipped in.

"No one's talking to you," I reminded her. "Anyway, haven't you got a home to go to?"

Sophie always fell for that one.

"I live here," she replied indignantly, "which is more than you do half the time. Anyway, haven't you got some homework to go to?"

"No, as a matter of fact, I'm still on holiday and we haven't been set our homework assignments yet, so why don't you crawl back under the paving stone you crawled out of."

"Abi!" everyone shouted.

"Okay, I'm sorry, but this is serious, Mum. If you can transmit thoughts could you also transmit energy?"

"Yes, I'm sure we all do."

"But if Trancer...let's say he was being used to transmit energy, do you think that could explain why he became drained of energy? Like he was when he turned into a zombie?"

"Abi, I really don't know," mum said, but I could tell she had caught the look in dad's eye that said "leave it", or words to that effect.

"Is that how you turned into a zombie?" Sophie muttered.

"Sophie!" we all shouted, and that for the time being was the end of it.

A few days later a letter came from Duncan, addressed to 'Paul, Fiona and Abigail Edwards'. Sophie wanted to know why she hadn't been included and I had to remind her there's no point in writing letters to people who can't read.

Dear Paul, Fiona and Abi,

Apologies for not getting back to you earlier re. my enquiries into the Canons. I've been up to my ears in sorting out our export sales in Germany, which are proving a nightmare because of the new EC regulations...but you probably know my views on that already.

As I expected, my original enquiries about the so-called 'car crash' drew a complete blank, and it was only in the last month that I had time to visit Stuttgart where, as you know, the Canons moved to.

Richard Canon and I appear to have (or have had in his case) a mutual friend... well, acquaintance in my case, called Hans

Schmidt, who I was able to get to see on my last night in Stuttgart. Schmidt was able to shed some very interesting light on the matter.

It seems that Richard died eighteen months after the Canons arrived in Stuttgart, possibly of a heart attack. Frances, widowed and alone in a foreign country with two young sons, was befriended by a couple of bereavement counsellors – and get this – the names of these wonderful warm-hearted sharing, caring people were none other than Gerald and Monica Polson.

The Polsons, it seems, are psychologists, and they have had their fingers in a lot of pies, research into ageing, genetics and so forth; they were also running one of those 'human development and personal growth' courses and raking in a lot of Deutschmarks by all accounts. They also seemed to have been dabbling in some kind of psychic research.

Anyway, as I said, they started counselling Frances for bereavement, but Natalie, the daughter (as of course you know), seems to have been peculiarly resistant to the Polsons' dubious charms. She may even have fallen out with her mother over their growing influence on the rest of the Canons.

Natalie may have returned to England

but it is more likely she decided to travel with the inheritance from Richard's will. After that, I'm afraid, Schmidt told me the trail went cold.

However, you may remember that I told you I had a colleague who works on *Der Spiegel*, and by chance he has located a paper cutting regarding the death of an unidentified woman in a Stuttgart apartment block two years after Richard's death. I am enclosing the cutting and leave it to you to decide what it means.

Schmidt had one final piece of information: "Steer clear of the Polsons," he warned me. "They're dangerous people. What's worse they have powerful connections in high places." I'm afraid he didn't elaborate.

Nettie sends her love and has asked me to remind Abi that she's welcome to come and stay any time.

Regards,

Duncan

The newspaper cutting was, of course, in German, which dad translated. All it said was that the body of the woman, who was believed to be in her early forties, had not been identified.

But what was more interesting was the accompanying photo of the police and ambulance taking away the body on a stretcher.

There, in the watching crowd, I could make out two figures who, though the photo was blurred, could have been the Polsons. They were holding hands with an older and younger boy.

The more I looked at the photo the more I was convinced that the two children were Jamie and Mark and that the two adults were the Polsons.

I looked from mum to dad, shocked at their complete lack of reaction.

"I knew they were lying," I said vehemently. "Can't we go to the police?"

"On this evidence?" dad said and shook his head. "They'd laugh at us. Abi, you've got to leave this thing alone."

I could have screamed. Couldn't they see how it all fitted? I was now sure that the Polsons had brought Jamie and Mark back to London and were keeping them prisoner in the house across the road from our old flat.

But how in that case could I have seen Jamie – or someone who looked exactly like Jamie – three times in different places?

There had to be a way to get to Jamie and Mark. What was happening in that house? What were the Polsons doing to them?

If Trancer really was Jamie, could it be the Polsons who were responsible for 'the bad things'? Was it because of the Polsons that the life had seemed to drain out of him?

I suddenly felt a terrible sense of something evil going on in that house.

And I knew that Jamie's life was in peril...

Chapter 6

Sixth form college was going to be very demanding. It wasn't just adapting to the new curriculum, more essays and more homework, but also adjusting to a new class. There would be new faces, students from different schools. Some of them I had seen around town, others were complete strangers.

I knew I should be starting to prepare my schoolwork, but all I could think about in the week before I went back was Jamie – or Trancer who looked like Jamie.

I was having strange dreams and once again I dreamt that Jamie and I were playing hide and seek in my old flat. The dream was almost a complete rerun of the one I'd had in France, except that this time as I fell through the gap in the floorboards I heard Trancer's voice saying "Somewhere down there...you've got the key...".

I woke up sweating and terrified, the words still ringing in my ears, and as I lay in bed thinking of the old days, I suddenly remembered.

I did have the key...or at least I knew where it might be.

Why hadn't I thought of it before?

I rang Nettie and reminded her of her offer to let me come and stay, without mum or dad or Sophie.

Nettie was delighted and not too surprised at my next question. No, Duncan still hadn't sorted out the nursery – my old bedroom. The baby was due in December and if he didn't get round to decorating it by the end of October they'd have to get the professionals in, although Duncan was convinced they were all cowboys. At least cowboys did the work when they said they would, she added sniffily. And yes, I could sleep in it if I didn't mind the mess.

I told mum and dad I was going to spend the day with Nettie. They raised an eyebrow or two and cautioned me to keep away from the Polsons and I said of course, I'd just like to spend a bit of time there and then they said well, don't bother Nettie too much and I said of course not... I don't like lying to my parents but I knew they would try to stop me going, especially because of what Duncan had said at the end of his letter.

In my shoulder bag I had packed a chisel, a small saw, hammer, torch and magnet. I hoped that was all I would need.

It was a Wednesday and I arrived at the flat at midday. Nettie made me very welcome and we sat and chatted for a while in her trendy wine-bar sitting room.

"It looks as though the Polsons must have persuaded that poor woman to give them the deeds of the house," she said, when I turned the subject to Duncan's letter. "Still, as you know, Duncan's friend thinks we should all steer clear of them and I hope you'll take his advice, Abi."

She looked at me narrowly for a few seconds and I felt distinctly uncomfortable.

"Don't worry, Nettie," I lied, "I'm not going to do anything stupid."

"I'm sure you're not," she replied, and for some reason I knew she had her doubts. But she didn't say any more about it and then she went off to do the shopping.

Immediately after she'd gone I sprang into action.

Even more junk had found its way into my old bedroom and it took me a full ten minutes to clear away the cardboard boxes and old furniture so that I had access to the floorboards along one wall.

I was relieved to find that the floorboards were in several pieces, which would make it easier for me to lift up and put back the one I needed. With the fork end of the hammer I yanked out the nails and prised up the loose board with the chisel; then I shone the torch along the filthy joists.

Dipping the magnet inside the gap, I slid it up and down the joists, fishing for loose bits of metal. To my satisfaction I felt and heard the tiny clinks as they jumped to the magnet. Eventually I pulled it out.

My heart sank as I pulled off the debris of filthy metal that clung to it. I felt like a fisherman who finds an old boot at the end of his rod.

Again I trawled the magnet under the floorboards. My misery increased when I drew out the magnet with only a couple of nails and a drawing pin stuck to it.

Then I shone the torch through the gap again. The quest seemed to have proved futile when, at the furthest end of the joist beneath, the torch beam picked up something that gleamed dully. Holding the magnet at the end of my fingertips, I stretched my arm down and along as far it would reach and held my breath.

Suddenly there was a small clank.

Gingerly, I pulled the magnet out.

I'd got it.

The rusty key must have lain there for eight years since the day Jamie dropped it by mistake through a hole in the floorboards while we were playing hide and seek.

"If you find it," Jamie had said all those years ago, "you can burgle my house – if you can get past Jonah."

Jonah, as you may remember me telling you, was the Canons' Jack Russell terrier who yapped a lot and terrorised the postman, but was otherwise harmless.

The Alsatian wasn't. I had no idea how I would get past Big Bad Jonah, but I'd made up my mind that I would cross that bridge when I came to it.

It was time to replace the floorboards. This would mean hammering and that meant I had to get it done quickly before Nettie got back – or before one of the tenants in the flat above or below turned up to complain.

The floorboards were back in place and the key safely in my jeans pocket by the time Nettie returned. She had said I could come and go as I pleased and not to worry about her, so I sat at my old bedroom window and waited.

I remembered what Nettie had said on our previous visit: the Polsons left the house every Wednesday between three and six. Today was Wednesday and at five past three I saw the Polsons' car emerge from their driveway.

I watched as the passenger window slid down and Mrs Munster opened the driveway gates with a remote control device. The gates swung shut as the car exited and I could see Polson in the driver's seat. They turned into the side road and I waited until the car disappeared up the hill.

I intended to leave thirty minutes before they returned, so I had exactly two and a half hours...

Chapter 7

I told Nettie I was going for a walk.

The house across the road where the Polsons now lived was at the corner of two roads: Somerset Road on which Duncan and Nettie lived and Farley Rise, where the Polsons had driven their car.

Farley Rise led uphill to a park and on the further side of the park was my old school. Sometimes mum or dad or Frances and occasionally Richard would drive Jamie and me up the hill to school, though more often we walked.

On the nearer side of the park was a network of back gardens and alleyways. If you had asked me to draw a map or give directions to anyone who wanted to get through this maze of alleys, I would have found it quite impossible.

But my feet or some other part of my anatomy seemed to remember instinctively, and having walked up the hill to the park I then wove my way through the alleys until I came to the garden that was next to Jamie's old house.

At the end of this garden there was a broken fence...still broken after seven years, I was relieved to discover. I climbed through it into an area of thick undergrowth.

In the midst of this was the clearing which Jamie and I had turned into our hidey hole.

I vaguely remembered that we had once

buried some 'treasure' there in a plastic bag. I would have liked to have dug it up but there was no time for that now.

The farthest side of the undergrowth was a mass of nettles, bushes and tangled branches, and as I approached it I could feel my heart beating faster.

Everything depended now on finding the gap in the fence of what used to be the Canons' driveway.

Would it still be there or would the Polsons have mended it? They were obviously very security conscious, as was proved by the surveillance cameras Sophie had spotted in the front garden.

I surveyed the little jungle of undergrowth and tried to estimate where the gap would have been. Glumly I realised it was probably where the waist-high nettles grew thickest. At least I was well covered in my jeans and jacket.

I put on my gloves and covered as much of my face and hair as possible in a scarf and waded in.

When I came to the fence I had to kneel down to look for the gap and in spite of all my protective gear I winced with pain as the nettles stung my cheeks. But all my attention was now concentrated on feeling for the gap.

As the minutes went by my dismay increased. The gap wasn't there! The Polsons must have patched the fence. How could I have been so naïve as to think otherwise!

In desperation I shoved my body forward through the nettles...and then felt something give. I had found it!

The hole was there, but in seven years a thick web of branches had grown round it. I yanked at the branches but they were so firmly embedded that I could hardly move them. Thankfully I remembered the saw I had packed in my shoulder bag.

It took another ten minutes before I had sawn enough of the branches to make a hole wide enough to push my body through. By this time I was sprawled on the ground, levering myself with the palms of my hands inch by inch through the gap, as the branches tore at my body.

My progress was painfully slow and I was breathing heavily. I knew that unless I put one massive effort into shoving myself through, it could take me hours. I rested for a minute and then, taking a deep breath, concentrated my mind on a last supreme effort.

I was through. I picked myself up and surveyed the damage. My jeans were ripped at the knees (could I pass this off as a fashion accessory?) and the top pocket of my jacket was torn, it could have been much worse. My hands were bruised and my face still smarted from the nettles, but I could live with that.

I gazed around me. I was now inside the Polsons' driveway, which had changed little from when the Canons lived there. This was separate from the front of the house where all the security was, although there was an alleyway connecting them, with a locked door in between.

At the corner of the back of the house, next to the garage, I knew there was an old door that used to open into the utility room which annexed the kitchen. The key that Jamie had dropped through my floorboards belonged to the lock in that door.

I prayed it still fitted.

I switched on my torch and stealthily inserted the key in the lock. For agonising seconds it didn't move. I remembered not to force it, but instead jangled the key in the lock.

At last it began to turn with a loud creak and I gently opened the door.

From within the house, probably in the hallway, I heard Big Bad Jonah begin to bark.

I was in the house, or at least in the utility room. I shone the torch along the room to the far door and tiptoed towards it. I could hear the barking growing louder.

To my horror I discovered that this door, too, was locked. Please, key, open this door, I muttered to myself.

But this time my luck had run out.

Worse, much worse, and what made my stomach churn, was the barking coming from the other side of the door.

I could almost see Big Bad Jonah in my mind's eye, crouched on all fours and slavering as he looked forward to his next meal.

If I did manage to get through the door I would have to act quickly to stop his next meal from being me.

I poked around at the bottom of my shoulder bag and finally found what I was looking for: a paperclip. For the next few, interminable minutes I fiddled with the lock, all the while having to endure BBJ's bloodcurdling barking that grew in volume as he became more excited.

My fingers were starting to tremble. Even if I did open the lock, how was I going to get past BBJ who I could already visualise pouncing on me and ripping me into tasty morsels?

I had almost given up trying to turn the lock when, partly to my relief and partly to my horror, it slowly started to slide open.

And on the other side of the door was BBJ...

Chapter 8

I had to think fast. I couldn't just walk through the door into the jaws of a vicious guard dog, but I couldn't just stay imprisoned in the utility room. There was only one thing I could do.

I stepped over to the inside edge of the door, where the hinges were, and stretched across to grasp the handle. As I turned the handle, I pulled the door open, swinging it right back so that I was hidden between the door and the wall. At the same time I threw the chisel from my shoulder bag right across to the far end of the utility room.

Barking furiously, Big Bad Jonah leapt into the room, tearing across to where he had heard the chisel crashing on the floor.

I didn't waste a moment.

Whipping through the door, I bolted it behind me. I was now in the kitchen, and behind me, back in the utility room, I could hear Big Bad Jonah going berserk, barking and dementedly lashing against the door with his paws.

I crept through the kitchen door into the hallway – at least that door was open, but all the lights were out. Before I switched on my torch I waited, listening for any sign of human life. But all I could hear was Big Bad Jonah, his barking now muffled between two closed doors.

And yet I was still convinced that somewhere in the house I would find Jamie and Mark, or at least evidence that they had been there recently.

I shone my torch along the hallway and then began to explore.

I'm not normally sensitive to atmospheres. Mum can go into a house and tell you whether the vibes are good or bad. That's how she chose our home in Swanleigh. She vetoed all the houses that dad liked, and in the end he always gave way.

In one house we went to when we were house-hunting she started crying and said that someone had died there in great pain. Later we found out that that was exactly what had happened.

I think I was able to feel the atmosphere in the Polsons' house because it was so different from what I had expected. After all those years I would still have recognised the Canons' atmosphere, like you might suddenly recognise someone you thought you'd completely forgotten about. But it had changed.

As I went from room to room – to my surprise most of them unlocked – I started to feel a strange tingling in my cheeks and fingertips and my head felt heavy, like you do before a thunderstorm. I can only describe the atmosphere as in some way electric. Perhaps all atmospheres are electric but we don't register them until there's something very different about them. And then we don't know how to measure them or describe them.

I didn't like it. It was what mum would have called a bad vibe.

However, I had got this far and I wasn't going to chicken out now. I needed to find some clue as to what was going on, what might have happened to Jamie and Mark.

Besides, while I've said the overall atmosphere had changed, every now and again I was beginning to pick up a sense of someone I felt close to.

I could feel Trancer.

Don't ask me how, but ever since the Phoenix Festival I had been having flashes, hardly thoughts or images, but more like sensations that came to me unexpectedly. I had come to recognise Trancer's frequency just like you might pick up the taste of vanilla in a dessert, or a guitarist whose sound you know, even though you didn't know you knew it, if you see what I mean.

In the back study I found shelves full of books – in German, Russian and English. Those I could identify – in other words, the ones in English – were on psychology, molecular biology, genetics and so on. There were other books on hypnotism, mind control and projection, and the development of psychic powers. There was even a shelf – and this made me shudder – on vampirism.

Could the Polsons be vampires?

The thought was preposterous. Vampires don't really exist. They're just something you get in horror films, like *Dracula*. Thomas, my ex-boyfriend, had really been into all that stuff.

I tried to imagine the Polsons drinking Jamie's blood. The thought was so horrible that I quickly shook my head to get rid of it. Now was not the time for me to be getting squeamish or over-sensitive.

I saw a large, walnut desk on which there was a computer whose screensaver was still running. One by one I went through all the drawers, rifling through letters and other documents for some sign of Jamie and Mark's presence in the house.

There was nothing.

I felt depressed and disheartened. There was only one other source of information in the room and I approached it nervously, wishing my dad was with me. He's a whizz at getting into programs and games and it was one thing he had in common with Thomas.

I've never really taken much interest, apart from using a word processor for my essays and notes, though I enjoy screen painting, which dad has given me a lot of help with as he's a graphic designer.

I pressed a key, knowing at least that that's how you get out of the screensaver, and my heart sank.

It was a bare screen apart from two words:

ENTER PASSWORD:

I sighed. It was hopeless. How on earth could I hope to guess what the Polsons might have chosen for a password?

I decided to do what we did at school when we started a new subject, which was called brainstorming. You just think of any idea, however bizarre and way out, that you associate with a subject, and it helps you to start thinking about it.

The trouble with brainstorming is it works best with a group of people so they can all contribute ideas. But now there was only me and my very little brain.

And then of course my little brain went a complete blank as it always does when I tell myself I have to use it.

I tried to relax my mind, which was what you're supposed to do, but all I could think was that it was now four-fifteen and I only had another hour or so before the Polsons would be coming back – if not before.

Come on, Abi, I told myself. Think.

I thought of all the words I could connect with the Polsons.

Polson, Polsons, Munsters, vampires, evil, surveillance, psychic, Trancer...

The image of Trancer floated back into my mind:

I'm a transmitter...transmission...trance mission...

I had nothing to lose.

I entered the word:

transmitter

I held my breath and pressed the return key.

INCORRECT

I sighed and had another go.

transmission

INCORRECT

I breathed deeply. I could spend the whole day doing this and not get anywhere.

Without even thinking I typed:

trance mission

In a flash the screen went blank.

I had failed.

Then, seconds later, to my astonishment the screen lit up in multicoloured graphics.

I had got the password!

I could hardly contain my excitement. I had felt all along that there was a connection between Trancer and Jamie. Now I knew for sure.

Maybe he had been guiding me to him ever since the day I saw Jamie dancing in the window. Perhaps he had even talked to me in my dreams. All the old questions about Jamie and Trancer returned to my mind, but now I might start to get some answers.

I looked at the screen and clicked on to SEARCH, then entered:

canon

There was a pause while the computer did the search and then a new screen came up.

CANON, JAMES WILLIAM: PROFILE

appeared at the top of the screen and underneath was Trancer's face, front and profile, in full-colour graphics.

It was not the happy, animated face I knew from Reading, nor the zombie he had turned into at the end of the day, but somewhere in between. He looked solemn and what little expression there was in his face seemed sad.

Beneath this were details such as his birth date, age, weight, blood type, blood pressure, pulse rate and even biorhythms and DNA analysis.

Oh, Jamie, I whispered to myself, what have they done to you?

I paged down and came to spreadsheets and graphs which at first seemed to me like complete gobbledygook. Then I examined the data more closely.

A series of numbers were listed in rows and columns, with dates and times in the left-hand column. The last date was today's. The headings above included: alpha and beta rhythms, brain performance indicators, fatigue factors, ECG and PSI ratings.

The bottom row of data was actually changing as I watched it.

On the next screen was something even more startling: there, moving up and down in regular waves, was a moving chart which I later discovered was called an electrocardiogram. This showed the strength and frequency of Jamie's heartbeats.

With a shock I realised that the screen was

monitoring a process that was going on at this moment somewhere in the house.

I paged to the next screen. This gave similar data for CANON, MARK GORDON. His face was less familiar and I had to remind myself that the last time I saw him he was six.

I checked my watch – it was four-forty. I had less than an hour left. I closed the file and switched it back to the original screen. It was time to go upstairs.

Chapter 9

As I had expected there were closed-circuit TV monitors in every room, but they were switched to surveillance of the outside.

I realised to my horror that there must have been more cameras in the garden because in one of the monitors I could clearly see our old house. I could even see my bedroom window.

I wondered if the Polsons had two sets of cameras, one set for outside surveillance and one for inside. Perhaps if the cameras spotted an intruder coming in from outside, the surveillance was switched to internal monitoring. And as I had got into the house through the back way, the internal monitors had not been switched on.

I had to believe this. It was my only hope.

Upstairs every room glowed with a pale blue light which was coming from the monitors. As I shone the torch tentatively towards a window I realised why the light couldn't be seen from outside. There was a thick, black blind blanketing out each window, shutting in the light.

Jamie must have pulled up the blind the night I saw him dancing at the window. He must have been crazy...out of his mind.

My search was proving futile. I seemed to have been in and out of every room twice and there was still no sign of either Jamie or Mark.

A new thought occurred to me. Was it

possible that the Polsons had smuggled the boys out in the back of the car?

No, something told me that they were here in the house. I was starting to feel their presence very strongly and I could no longer tell the difference between this feeling and the one I had experienced earlier about Trancer's presence.

Then I remembered the electrocardiogram which I had seen plotting the boys' heartbeats. What further proof did I need that Jamie and Mark were somewhere very nearby? I had to find them.

The time was now five o'clock. I had exactly thirty minutes.

I returned downstairs and stood in the hallway, trying to think. Big Bad Jonah had quietened down in the utility room, but he was still giving the occasional bark and growl. And I had yet to work out how I was going to get out of the house without being torn to pieces by him.

Was there another room I had overlooked? Again I tried to think. Where did we used to play?

Once again I recalled the dream in which Jamie and I played hide and seek and the awful falling sensation as I descended through the floorboards.

That's where I come from...somewhere down there...

And at the same moment I remembered the muffled cry that seemed to come from under the house while Sophie and I were talking to Polson.

Of course! How could I have forgotten! The playroom was in the cellar. How could I have blocked out that memory?

I knew the answer.

I didn't block it out. Polson did!

It was just after Sophie and I heard the cry from the cellar, that Polson had said those words that seemed to mesmerise us.

Impossible…impossible…lamplight… lamplight…leaves…leaves…shadows… shadows …imagine…imagine…imagine…imagine…

No wonder I had forgotten!

I tiptoed towards the cellar door below the staircase. As I approached it I saw the black number pad and realised to my dismay that it was a combination lock. My chances of stumbling on the combination and opening the door were infinitesimal.

Above the pad was a small, glass peephole. Leaning forward, I peered through it.

My heart began to pound and my chest felt so tight I could hardly breathe.

For the first few moments my mind could hardly register what I was seeing…and when it did I started back in horror…

Nothing could have prepared me for the extraordinary scene I had just witnessed: through the fisheye lens I made out an ultramodern computer lab. In the eerie artificial light, two boys were sitting rigidly still at a long, black workstation desk, both of them hooked up to what looked like virtual reality headsets. Occasionally they moved a joystick, but mainly – and what made my blood run cold – they were frozen like zombies in a VR trance, their faces pale, lifeless, completely without expression.

A spaghetti of wires was hooked from their heads and bodies to a stack of black machines.

What did this remind me of?

I remembered Trancer at the end of the day in Reading as he was transformed in front of my eyes into a lifeless zombie, and I knew without a shadow of a doubt that the older of the two boys was Trancer.

And I also knew that Trancer was Jamie.

But another, much older, memory came into my mind. It floated back to me across the years.

Jamie and I were seven years old and for our school Christmas play we had taken the parts of Kay and Gerda in Hans Andersen's *The Snow Queen*.

Jamie was Kay, who sat in the Snow Queen's frozen palace, rigid and cold, making 'Ice Puzzles of Reason'. The Snow Queen had entranced him so that he was blind to everything but solving puzzles made out of ice, because of the splinter of glass which had come from the 'Devil's mirror' and had got into his eye.

I was Gerda, who had set out to rescue him and after a lot of adventures had finally managed to find him in the Snow Queen's palace while she was away.

But Kay didn't respond to Gerda, and it was only when she was so upset that she began to cry and shed hot tears that penetrated Kay's heart and thawed the little bit of mirror in him, that Kay recognised her.

But at this moment, I had no tears to cry. I was too horrified, too numb. Instead I found myself shrieking, "Jamie!".

He didn't react, didn't turn.

There was nothing I could do. Nothing more I could say.

I don't know how long I stayed there transfixed at the view, but I suddenly realised that I had very little time left before the Polsons were due to return and yet I was still feeling too weak and dazed to move.

As I tried to pull myself together I was reminded of the fact that I would have to leave the same way I came in.

From the utility room I could hear BBJ give a long, low growl.

Chapter 10

Somehow I would have to make my escape. Still trembling with the shock of what I had just seen, I made my way back along the hallway to the kitchen, beyond which was the utility room and suddenly froze in my tracks.

I had just realised that when I opened the utility room door, BBJ would charge out at me, but this time – unlike before when I had been able to swing the door round and hide behind it – I would be unable to do so.

Because the door only opened one way... and that was back into the utility room. This time I would have no place to hide...

I thought of my options. The most obvious was to leave by the front door but I instantly ruled that out. I would never get past the surveillance cameras: I had visions of alarms going off, police arriving...the Polsons had friends in high places. Besides, I already knew that it would be impossible to open that thick steel front gate which was obviously connected to the security system.

The other downstairs exit was via the garage but as I had seen from the front security system and the remote control of the driveway gates, I knew that opening the garage doors would be electronically controlled. I would be as much a prisoner in the garage as in the front garden.

I thought of getting out through an upstairs

window and sliding down a drainpipe. But this option was even more ridiculous: I had no head for heights and the very thought of it made me feel dizzy and nauseous.

The fourth alternative was to find a place to hide until BBJ was safely out of the utility room. But then again I might have the three of them to contend with.

There was one more option and that was simply to open the utility room door and brave BBJ.

However crazy it might sound now, I decided this was what I was going to do. At that moment I just wanted to get out of the house before the Polsons returned and I wanted to believe that I could still win BBJ round by gentle handling.

As I crossed the kitchen I heard the Alsatian growling from behind the bolted door. Nervously I unbolted the door, knowing that he could now be just feet away. With a shaking hand I pushed the door open...

Big Bad Jonah was crouched in the middle of the utility room. Instantly he jumped up, barking furiously. Hardly believing what I was doing, I knelt down so that I was level with him. This seemed to have some effect because, instead of springing at me, he stood fixed to the spot, baring his teeth and growling.

I would like to say I stood my ground and made friends with him, but the truth is I was quickly losing my nerve, especially as I could see he was very hungry and, still growling and salivating, was beginning to approach me.

I felt my heart pounding as I edged away, backing out of the kitchen into the hall. I was now certain that any second he would leap on me...

I could see him tense, getting ready to spring and I backed away further. He was about to jump at me, when I collided into something big, solid and immovable behind me.

To my amazement and relief, BBJ lay down on his haunches and whimpered obediently.

Swinging round, I found myself face to face once more with Jamie – but not my friend of many years ago, nor the dancing boy in the window, nor Trancer as I had seen him at the Phoenix Festival and had got to know at Reading.

His face was set like granite. He didn't even appear to see me.

"Jamie...I–"

A voice came roaring into my head, like a train approaching out of a tunnel. Get out...go away...we don't need you...

The voice grew to an ear-splitting crescendo until I had to put my fingers in my ears. And yet Jamie remained motionless and said nothing. He looked past me at Big Bad Jonah who almost casually, reluctantly, stood up and walked past me to a smaller figure who was standing behind him.

It was Mark Canon.

I found it almost impossible to recognise in this impenetrable figure the little imp who used to giggle and fight with Sophie in the back of Fran's car. What would she think of her darling little Marky now, I wondered.

Because, while Jamie seemed vacant, rigid, like stone, there was something threatening and malevolent in the way Mark's concentrated stare seemed to laser through me. It reminded me of Polson's drilling gaze and I felt I had no way of protecting myself from it.

You are not wanted here...

The voice that was roaring in my head, making it hard for me to think, was harsh and unyielding.

How could you let them do this to you, Marky? I found myself thinking, as though I now had no alternative but to respond to him telepathically, as mum would have put it.

And even though I felt cold waves of terror sweeping over me, I still found in myself a small, safe area where I could talk to myself and try to reason out what was happening.

I knew as long as I stayed in this safe room the voice couldn't harm me. I even started to picture the room: it was like our sitting room used to be in London and I saw mum and dad sitting there and some of my friends from school; I even allowed Sophie to come in as long as she kept her trap shut.

We were all laughing at the voice, like Sophie and I sometimes used to do when we stayed up and watched a really bad late-night horror film in black and white from the 1950s. And then I knew that it was mum I needed to talk to.

The conversation that followed between me and mum in my safe room, which I will try to relate as accurately as I can, took only a few seconds of real time, but I experienced it in what I later decided to call 'safe-room time' which I believe is much slower. I think it was the very fear I was feeling which must have opened the door that led me into that room.

— What's going on, Mum? I asked her in my mind.

— I'm not sure, Abi, she replied, in that gentle, thoughtful way of hers, but I've got the feeling that Mark especially has become the prime target for psychic programming. After all, Polson got him when he was young.

— How can I help Mark? Can't I do something?

— Not now, Abi, not yet. But maybe...

— What?

— Well, it's occurred to me that more than fifty per cent of the will being exerted against you is coming from Mark. I think Jamie would like to be free and has had to find a way of escaping from the Polsons in his mind. And when he escapes he becomes Trancer.

— Do you mean Trancer wasn't really there at the Phoenix and at Reading?

— I think he was there, in his mind. He was

able to go there because of you.

— How do you mean?

— This is what I think, Abi, and I may be wrong. I think both boys have an unusual psychic potential.

— You mean psychic power?

— Yes, and I think that the Polsons have been exploiting this for their own purposes. They have been force-feeding Jamie and Mark psychic energy.

— Come again?

— Do you remember Hansel and Gretel, when the witch feeds them up?

— So that she can eat them? Are the Polsons going to eat them?

— No, not physically, but they are feeding off their psychic energy.

— And that's why the boys were hooked to the machines?

— Yes, it's a bit like the way they battery-farm chickens. They're being forced day after day to raise the levels of their psychic power.

— And is that how Jamie was able to travel in his mind?

— Yes, he has the ability, but it is also his escape. In order to travel he became Trancer. But Trancer doesn't know Jamie and Jamie doesn't know Trancer.

— He doesn't know he's doing it?

— I think he's starting to. I think the two halves of Jamie and Trancer are starting to connect.

— But if he wasn't really there, physically, how was Lizzie able to see him as well as me?

— Through you, Abi: you are his lifeline and Lizzie saw him because you did.

— So what can I do to help Jamie now?

— Invite Trancer into the safe room now and introduce him to Jamie.

In my mind I did as she told me. I opened the door and let Trancer in. He walked in grinning, did a couple of somersaults and then danced around the room before looking contrite and a little embarrassed.

— It's okay, Trancer, these are all my family and friends, they want to help you, I said.

Then I brought in Jamie. In comparison he seemed inert, lifeless, but even in my safe room I could sense his power – a power that had been turned in on itself, like a muscle-bound athlete.

— Jamie, I said, looking towards mum for support, I want you to meet Trancer. Trancer is you, Jamie, the part of you that wants to be free of all this.

At first the Jamie who walked into my safe room didn't respond, but then he began to stare at Trancer as if at a ghost, as though he'd woken up from a long sleep and was staring at himself in the mirror and could hardly recognise what he saw, but knew in his heart that it was his own reflection.

Then his expression changed again. He was growing agitated and his face began to contort in a scream of agony and remorse.

And all the while Trancer remained serene, unperturbed, unaware of the effect he was having, happy as before to be oblivious of 'the bad things'.

As Jamie began to scream, the floor of the safe room started to shudder and shake as in an earth tremor. Once again Mark's voice came roaring into my head and the safe room dissolved.

Go now...we don't need you...you are not wanted here.

I found myself backing away again, this time towards the kitchen, but as I did so I could see a change in Jamie – not the Jamie in my safe room, but the real flesh and blood Jamie who was standing in front of me.

I could swear that he too, like safe room Jamie, was waking up.

"Abi?" he said, in a thick, troubled voice. He looked lost and bewildered.

Go now... The voice was continuing to thunder in my head.

"Jamie!" I pleaded, desperately wishing that I could drag him away with me, but by now it was impossible for me to resist the magnetic force that was repelling me away from him.

"I'm a transmitter, Abi!" Jamie shouted, screwing up his fists as though he were fighting a voice within himself – or was it also emanating from Mark?

You mean nothing to us...get out...

"Help me, Abi!" Jamie gasped. "Help us..."

But I knew that his voice and will were

growing weaker as Mark's voice grew stronger.

"I'll get help, Jamie, I promise," I shouted back as I felt myself propelled towards the utility room.

I was dimly aware that I still had to relock the door between the utility room and the kitchen, but where was the paperclip? My hands were shaking and I doubted whether I would have had the ability to do it anyway.

But then to my amazement I heard the lock turn. How could that be when seconds earlier I had seen Jamie and Mark standing at the far side of the hall?

Of course I knew the answer: it was Mark who was using his mind power to lock the door. But I had no time to wonder further about the nature of that power.

From outside in the driveway I could hear the Polsons' car pulling up in the driveway and preparing to enter the garage.

I had no choice but to crouch behind an old cupboard in the utility room. I heard the garage door shut and then the Polsons' voices only a few feet away. If I were to escape, now was my only chance.

A disturbing thought now came to me: would the boys – would Mark – squeal on me? Maybe they wouldn't need to. Maybe Polson would know.

As I crouched in the darkness I wondered what the extent of his psychic power was? Somehow I sensed that it was limited – that while he could exert his will and use hypnotic control, he did not have the same gift to read minds, transmit thoughts or to travel in his mind like Jamie and Mark. The Polsons could feed off their psychic energy but they couldn't generate it themselves. That was why they needed the boys.

I sensed and knew all this without actually consciously thinking it, just as the conversation between me and mum in the safe room had happened on some intuitive level that was different from the normal exchange of thoughts and ideas.

I heard their voices recede into the house and then I slipped out of the back door. Locking it behind me and creeping to the back of the driveway, I slipped out the way I had come in.

Five minutes later I was back on the pavement outside the Polsons' house. As I was about to cross the road and return to the flat I glanced back.

Look at me, Abi, I'm dancing!

Jamie was back at the window. The light was on. The blind was up and once again he was dancing. Out of his body. Out of his mind.

Oh God, Jamie, what are you doing? I said to myself and then it occurred to me that this was Trancer again – Jamie's other half – and that although I could see him, the Polsons couldn't.

But seconds later, I began to wonder. For behind Jamie/Trancer I saw a shadow, the silhouette of Polson as he entered the room.

The light went off. The blind was pulled down.

I suddenly knew with an awful certainty that Jamie Canon had begun the process of consciously acting out the rebellion of his secret, unconscious half, Trancer...and that his life was now in terrible danger...

Chapter 11

I stood on the grey pavement feeling the chill of the early September evening creeping into my bones and gazed at the front of the house for I don't know how long, watching the blacked-out bedroom window.

Why was I waiting? For Jamie to reappear at the window? Or to come running out of the house, greeting me with some awful quip , then trundling up the hill together to school like we had at the beginning of a new autumn term seven years ago?

I was so lost in reverie, trying to reconcile my recent appalling encounter with the boy I used to know, who had made me a mouse's head and read my eyes and done the Moonwalk, that I didn't notice the front door open.

"Ah, you must be looking for your young friend again."

My blood froze. I felt as though a very large building – say, the size of your average Transylvanian castle – had fallen onto my head and I couldn't think, let alone speak or move.

Polson was standing at the door smiling benevolently at me. At least I think he meant it to appear benevolent but if skin could actually crawl, my skin would have been crawling along the South Circular Road at sixty miles an hour.

"Perhaps it would be a good idea if you came in. Then I might be able to convince you that your...what was his name?"

"Jamie..." I managed to say.

"Ah yes, Jamie...he is not here of course, but I don't think you will believe me unless you see for yourself."

I was slowly starting to be able to think again. At least I had recovered enough from the initial shock to realise that the surveillance cameras must have spotted me. How ironic that I had managed to break into their house, evade their security, escape their guard dog, hack into their computer and locate Jamie and Mark and yet here, out on the street, I had been picked out by their cameras.

What was I to do? If I refused to go in it would be inconsistent with my presence there today and my previous request to see the boys. He might suppose that I was devious, or frightened, or suspicious, and the Polsons might tighten their security even more.

What had he to gain from my coming into the house?

Was he planning to abduct me as well? I couldn't imagine so. From everything I had learned, from the details in Duncan's letter about the Polsons' early interest in the boys and the elaborate system that had been set up around them, it was obvious that the Polsons were not into random kidnapping. It would serve no purpose to kidnap me or kill me. My presence would be missed and suspicion could easily fall on them.

On the contrary, I decided that this was more likely to be a public relations exercise: they would have good reason to imagine that I had told other people of my suspicions that Jamie and Mark were in the house. So if they could convince me that the boys weren't there, they could relax in the knowledge that their security was assured.

What had I to lose? I might be able to find out something new, pick up further clues about what the Polsons were using the boys for. And maybe, just maybe, I would be able to get to Jamie again, before the blanket over his mind came down again, like the blanket his mother used to put over the telly when Michael Jackson's *Thriller* video came on so as not to scare little Mark...

And all the while another far more disturbing thought was going on in the back of my mind, like those subsonic hums you get in horror movies when the director is signalling to the audience that something really nasty is about to happen.

Maybe all the reasons I was giving myself for returning to the house now with the Polsons were coming from them! Maybe Polson was planting in my mind a compulsion to go back in and all my reasons...excuses?...were the result of hypnotic suggestion.

For all the time I had been hesitating he had been fixing me with those cold blue eyes and I had no power to resist.

I had to obey him.

The Entryphone buzzer sounded and the gate swung open. I felt myself almost being pulled up the garden path towards Polson and as I did so my head began to grow heavy again and I felt once more that tingling in my cheeks and fingertips, as though thunder was in the air...

"As you will see...Abigail, isn't it...we have a quiet little house here. Unfortunately my wife and I are childless, but as we are psychologists we know a little about young children."

From the kitchen I could hear BBJ barking again.

"...and dogs." He smiled. "Dogs are just like children, you know. They need a certain amount of training in obedience, just as we human beings need the correct education and mental discipline to train the mind."

He opened the door to the front living room. I had been in here earlier and noticed even more this time just how sterile and unlived-in it felt, like the fake living rooms you get in the furniture departments of large stores. There was a three-piece suite comprising a long, black Chesterfield sofa and two smaller, black leather armchairs, onto one of which he gestured for me to sit. I noticed a grandfather clock in one corner, and a couple of reproduction Georgian cabinets with glass doors that displayed various pieces of bric-a-brac.

"Ah," he said, as he saw me staring at an

object shaped like a tall cross with a loop on the top. "That is an ankh. It comes from Egypt and it is a very powerful symbol of eternal life.

"This Jamie of yours sounded an interesting fellow. You must have had quite a soft spot for him. Maybe you were sweethearts–"

"I didn't say that..." I said angrily.

"But it occurs to me that you had not seen him for some years and then of course, as I understand it, he died in a car crash."

I was tempted to call him a liar but thought better of it. I couldn't tell him that I had seen Jamie less than an hour earlier in the cellar and then in the hallway.

"Did he, perhaps, write to you or get in touch some other way, perhaps in a dream?"

"I told you last time, I saw him dancing...in the window."

"So you did, so you did..."

I started to feel dizzy under this interrogation, as though I were a patient in the adolescent unit of a mental hospital and he was the psychiatrist. He stood above me – towered above me – and every now and then he would start to pace.

"Would you say there was anything unusual about him?"

"I don't know what you mean."

Although of course I did.

"Could he, for instance, have had the power to communicate to you from beyond the grave? Do you remember his having psychic gifts?"

"I've told you, I saw him in the window. I know he isn't dead!"

I had decided that it was best to stick to my original story for consistency's sake, but I couldn't let him know that I had seen the boys inside the house.

"So you've seen him again, since the time when you saw him, as you say 'dancing in the window'? This interests me very much. My wife and I have a deep interest in the paranormal and it seems that your Jamie may indeed be a ghost."

I was surprised that he had gone so far as to admit at least this much about his interest in psychic research, but his questions were all angled in such a way as to make me believe he thought Jamie was dead.

I knew of course that was a lie. But all the same, I couldn't see why he was asking me these questions. After all, he must already know the power of Jamie and Mark's minds as he had been working on them for the past few years.

Could all this be a diversionary and delaying tactic while Mrs Munster cleared out all evidence of Jamie and Mark's presence and disposed of it into some nether region of the house that I wasn't aware of?

But then I realised the thought was preposterous. The boys must be locked securely in the cellar and the Polsons were hardly going to be escorting me around their computer lab. They would only let me see what they wanted me to see.

And then suddenly I could see the purpose of all the questions. Polson wanted to know if Jamie had the power to escape his influence. His power over Jamie had its limits and where those limits ended, which was when Jamie appeared to me as Trancer, that's where he couldn't go.

I don't know how I guessed all this, but it came to me in a flash and just as it did I could sense Polson's mind switching gears as it had done on the doorstep the first time I talked to him. Once again I felt the sensation that he was drilling into my head, trying to take control of my thoughts.

But this time I had a place to go where I could protect myself against him.

With a huge effort of will I turned my head away from his and looked down into my lap. But as I started to conjure up the safe room I felt the full force of Polson's own will. It was different from protecting myself against the voice that semeed to have emanated from Mark. That voice was like when you tuned the radio into one station, which was your own mind, your own thoughts, and another station emitting a stronger signal threatened to drown out the first station.

By going into my safe room I had been able to listen to my own mind; I could still hear Mark's 'voice' but I had been able to stop listening to it.

But when Polson began drilling into my mind I couldn't hear another station; he wasn't transmitting another signal, he wasn't a transmitter, he was an amplifier. It was more like he had control of the volume knob, so he could shut down my thoughts, but at the same time he was also able to fill my mind with black, sticky treacle which was how I imagined the content of his mind to be.

I concentrated on the safe room and imagined that me and my family and friends were painting the floor, walls and ceiling with thick, gold paint that was able to seal it off from Polson's cloying will.

I was aware that he was still talking, but his voice now seemed to bombard my mind in waves, like the waves of pain you get when you have toothache. When the pain was at its most acute I imagined I was at home in bed, with the cover over my head, hiding from the thunder, and mum was saying:

— Don't worry, Abi, it can't hurt you. It will pass. You're quite safe.

I looked up. The assault had passed. I could think again. It felt like a victory.

"So if you have had a visitation it would be of the utmost interest to us for you to let us know," he was saying, but I sensed he was disappointed, perhaps even slightly baffled, that he had been unable to dominate my thoughts.

"So much for the spectre of your deceased friend. Now, perhaps, I can demonstrate the physical evidence that he is not here by conducting you on a short guided tour. If you will come this way..."

He beckoned me to the door and then led me from room to room. To my surprise there was no sign of the surveillance monitors in the upstairs rooms.

I was starting to wonder what had happened to Mrs Munster when she suddenly loomed out of the darkness on the landing, rather like one of those skeletons that swing out at you on a ghost train.

"Perhaps it's time for our young visitor to be leaving," she said and I could hear the tension in her voice. "I'm sure your parents will be getting worried."

"I'm not staying with my parents," I replied without thinking and then caught the look that passed between them.

"So...you seem rather young to have left home," Polson said. "You are with relatives, friends of the family maybe?"

I cursed myself for having slipped up so badly. It was obvious they were fishing for information and I wasn't going to let them imagine that if I went missing no one would notice.

"Something like that," I replied firmly, remembering that knowledge is power. They weren't going to get any more out of me. Instead I said:

"Could I see the cellar?"

I don't know what made me say it. Perhaps I

wanted to call their bluff and see their reaction. But mostly it was pure frustration that they could imagine they could simply bamboozle me into thinking Jamie and Mark weren't there.

Again I caught the glance that flitted between them.

"The cellar?" Mrs Munster said in surprise. "Why do you want to go there?"

I bottled out somewhat and replied rather feebly, "We used to play there...I thought it would be nice to see it again...it would bring back the memories."

To my amazement, Polson smiled. "Very well, we will go and look in the cellar."

He turned and started walking down the stairs from the upper landing to the hallway. I followed between him and Mrs Munster, my insides churning as I realised that the moment of truth had arrived. How, in the time I had been talking to Polson, would Mrs Munster have possibly been able to get rid of the computer laboratory, let alone any signs of Jamie and Mark?

Where else could they be?

As Polson approached the cellar door, he pulled a bunch of keys from his jacket.

"I hope I still have the key," he muttered. "We don't often go down there."

Liar, liar, liar, I thought, but I was still baffled. Why bother with this charade when he was about to reveal the truth to me?

He pulled out an old rusty key and to my

surprise unlocked a padlock that I couldn't remember seeing on the cellar door earlier.

It suddenly struck me: the combination lock had disappeared.

The door slowly opened and I had to stifle a gasp of amazement.

Instead of the computer lab, I was staring down into a black hole: the smell of damp cobwebs hung from dank, mildewed rafters. Several of the steps were missing and all I could make out at the bottom were bags of rubble, pieces of broken furniture, an old mattress, the remains of a dismantled lawnmower.

It was a typical disused cellar.

"And now I think as you have seen everything there is to see," said Polson, "it is time to say goodbye. Thank you for our most interesting talk."

He barely concealed the disdain in his voice as he led me back to the front door.

"As you can see, your Jamie is no longer dancing in windows."

He pressed a button by the study door and the outside gate opened.

"Do give my regards to your...family friends."

Chapter 12

"What on earth have you been doing?" Nettie said, looking me up and down with a mixture of curiosity and alarm.

I couldn't blame her. I looked a mess with my ripped jeans and jacket and I guessed that she was already wondering what she was going to say to mum and dad.

"Oh, I went for a run and I...tripped on some barbed wire...I'm okay, really, Nettie, honestly I am."

She looked dubious but said tactfully, "Well, you probably want a bath. There's a dressing gown in the bathroom. I'll see what I can do about your clothes. I'll fix you a cup of tea – or would you prefer hot chocolate?"

"Thanks, Nettie, chocolate would be great."

I beamed at her and gave her a kiss. I was on the verge of bursting into tears and telling her everything, but that would have been a total disaster so I quickly made my exit and sank gratefully into a hot bath.

Everything was churning around in my mind and I had to decide what to do next.

Was I going mad? Could I have imagined seeing Jamie and Mark in the cellar? And yet... the cellar I had just seen bore no resemblance to the old playroom, any more than it did to the computer lab.

It didn't make sense.

And then, all at once, it did.

The cellar had been partitioned. It had always been so, even when the Canons lived there.

There were two cellars with an entrance door from the hallway and a second door immediately to the left of the landing inside this doorway, which opened to a second staircase leading down to the old playroom. The Polsons must have painted it black, which was why I hadn't seen it in the dark. As for the combination lock, it must have been subtly masked.

They had duped me and it only strengthened my resolve to rescue Jamie and Mark. And this time I wouldn't be going in on my own...

By the time I got out of the bath, all pink and shiny, I'd worked out a ground plan.

Nettie was brilliant. She'd fixed the ripped pocket of my jacket but left the hole in the knee of my jeans – "you might want to keep it this way". Then at my request, she rang my parents and told them I wanted to stay one more day and then handed the 'phone over to me, and dad said I hope you're steering clear of the Polsons and I said of course and then mum said you're not bothering Nettie and I said of course not and so on.

After a quick meal with Nettie, I excused myself and went back to the bedroom. For the rest of the evening I watched the house across the road from my window, thinking of the day's events and wondering how Jamie was. But there was no further sign of life from the house.

The next morning I rang my old London friend Chrissie Somers – she was the one who used to be my best friend and then wasn't and then was again and so on – and she still lived half a mile away. Her dad was a vet and I used to take the cats to his surgery for their injections. We arranged to meet up with Chrissie's older brother Col that afternoon at his flat in west London.

There was something I had to do first though, and that was look for some buried treasure...

How could I begin to explain what had gone on? I started at the beginning, which was when I had seen Jamie dancing in the window, and told them everything.

"I can't go to the police. Like my dad says, they'd laugh at me. But even Dad doesn't know the half of it. You should have seen them, Chrissie, they weren't the same. They were like ...robots...at least Mark was, but I think Jamie's trying to free himself."

"And that's where Trancer fits in? You think Trancer is actually Jamie's alter ego?" Col asked.

"I don't know, but I think when I first saw Jamie dancing in the window I was seeing Trancer, I mean, I was seeing the part of Jamie that was able to free himself."

"But why was Jamie dancing at the window?" asked Chrissie.

"I think I know, but it's hard to explain. It's like there's a part of him that he's protected, that Polson hasn't got to, and then sometimes he just finds himself in another place."

"Like at the window," said Chrissie.

"Or at festivals. I know you'll think I'm crazy but I believe he is able to get out of his body and go places."

"You mean like astral travel?" said Col.

"I think that's what it is. I've heard my mum talk about that. The thing is, I'm sure Trancer didn't know who he was...that he was actually a part of Jamie but then in a way he was giving me clues...leading me to find Jamie. And now I've seen Jamie I know he has started to become aware that he is also Trancer. So when I saw Jamie dancing in the window again yesterday, I think this time it really was Jamie, the physical Jamie and not just his Trancer projection."

"And what about Mark?" Chrissie asked.

"I don't know. I keep remembering that little boy of six...you remember him, Chrissie?"

She nodded.

"I still think he's in there, but he's become mentally powerful and I don't know if he still has the same personality underneath. I want to believe he has. I want to think that if we can get them both away from the Polsons, Mark will remember who he is."

"But you think Jamie's more in touch with himself?"

"Definitely. And he could also be the one

who can rescue Mark."

"So what do you think the Polsons are using them for?" Chrissie asked.

I hesitated. I'd thought a lot about this and I still remembered snatches of the 'conversation' I'd had with mum in the safe room.

"This is going to sound pretty weird and far out, but when I was in their study I saw all these books on vampires."

I saw Chrissie and Col exchange sceptical glances. "So you think the Polsons are vampires? They're drinking their blood?"

"No, not their blood. But I think they're feeding off their psychic energy."

Col whistled. "Psychic vampires! Yeah, that sounds reasonable. In a far out sort of way."

I sighed. "I didn't expect you to believe it. I know you must think I'm imagining it, but if you'd seen them in that basement...and the way Mark was able to get into my mind...and if you'd met the Polsons...I know they're somehow controlling it all, the Polsons I mean."

Then I told them what mum had said to me in the safe room about how she thought Jamie and Mark were being forced to boost their psychic power like battery chickens or Hansel and Gretel.

Col smirked. "And the Polsons are going to pop them in the oven and eat them."

"No, they're feeding off their psychic energy. That explains why Trancer suddenly went dead on me. That must have been when the Polsons were drawing on his energy. Like you drain a battery."

They still looked sceptical but I knew I was getting through to them.

So I told them my plan. Col worked for a computer company in London where he was a programmer. He also happened to be the oldest friend of Natalie Canon, Jamie and Mark's sister.

"She actually got in touch with me a few weeks ago," he said. "She came back to London last month and we were talking about meeting up. I could ring her now if you like."

I nodded eagerly. It was just what I was hoping to hear.

After he had rung her, Col got out his camcorder and videoed me. I spoke to Jamie and Mark, and I even spoke to Trancer, but afterwards I couldn't remember what I said, except that all my words seemed to come out in a rush and probably didn't make any sense and at the end of the video, before he switched off the camcorder, I was in tears.

Natalie came over to Col's flat an hour later. Of course she was much older-looking than the last time I had seen her; her face deeply tanned – not just the type you get from a fortnight on the Costa Brava, but from spending many years abroad in a hot climate.

She had lost a lot of weight – I think she'd got food poisoning in India – but it suited her. It was funny, though, how now I was sixteen and she was twenty-four I felt on much more equal terms with her than when I was nine and she sometimes baby-sat me and Soph.

She was obviously desperate to hear of any news about Jamie and Mark. Looking at her face I could see Jamie's features: the turned-up nose and wide, cheeky mouth. But her hazel eyes, edged with fine lines, had a hint of sadness in them and I wondered at all the experiences she had been through in the past seven years.

She listened in horrified silence as I told her my story and immediately promised to do anything she could to help. Then she started to talk about the Polsons.

"You probably know how they were psychologists and I think my father knew them casually – they were part of a small ex-patriot community in Stuttgart.

"I couldn't stick him from the start. I felt there was something very creepy about him and as for her – well, you've met her–"

"Mrs Munster's what Sophie and I called her."

Natalie smiled. "Yes, but at least Mrs Munster has a sense of humour. She's like a cross between a bossy headmistress and the priestess in some black magic cult. You want to laugh at them, but they're scary..."

"I know what you mean," I said.

"Anyway, Polson started coming round to our apartment, and then they both came. They used to ask questions about Jamie and Mark and kept saying what bright kids they were and how they'd be delighted to give them extra tuition as highly gifted children often needed extra stimulus, as they put it.

"They would take them out on what they called 'educational trips', and I suppose I didn't really notice it at first but later it was obvious that they were influencing them–"

"How?" Col asked.

"It's hard to say. Both my brothers are...were ...really high-spirited, they were always fooling around – well, you know, Abi."

I nodded.

"Anyway, after a few months they started becoming withdrawn at home, morose and sometimes, well, you know what kid brothers and sisters are like, they can be appalling."

I thought of Sophie and had to agree wholeheartedly.

"But this was different...they were becoming callous and sort of impenetrable. It was like they needed to exert their will over us. I had this definite feeling that they'd been got at–"

"By the Polsons," said Chrissie.

Natalie nodded. "And they seemed to be exercising more and more of a hold on them. Mum was uncomfortable about it, but Dad didn't seem to notice.

"But I remember just before Dad died that he seemed to have fallen out with them and I've always wandered whether they might not have had something to do with his having a heart attack."

106

TRANCE MISSION

"So you think they might have deliberately murdered your father?" Col asked.

"I've got no concrete evidence. It's just a feeling that they would never let anyone get in their way. But as you know, after his death, they started to give Mum bereavement counselling and she started relying on them. And then they persuaded her to let them educate Jamie and Mark themselves.

"I was finding it impossible to live in the apartment and it was mainly because of the Polsons that I decided to travel. I did have some money when Dad died, though not a lot because the Polsons had persuaded Mum to put a lot of her inheritance into an educational trust fund for the boys which they would administer.

"So I left Germany and went to Australia and then Thailand, and after that I lived in an ashram in India.

"I used to write to Mum but I never got a reply. And then when I finally returned to Stuttgart I heard of her death. After that I decided to come back to London to sort out my life and see if I could find out what had happened to Jamie and Mark.

"Well, now I know. It never occurred to me that they would be back at the old house..."

She stopped, her eyes full of tears, and I hugged her.

"Don't worry, Natalie," I said as we clung to each other, "we'll get them back."

Natalie had brought with her a large package

and she gave this to Col. Today was Thursday and school started in a week's time.

We arranged to meet up in a café up the road from Nettie's flat on Wednesday at two o'clock.

That left Col five days to prepare his box of tricks.

Before we parted, Natalie said, "There's something else I should tell you which I've only just remembered.

"One night when the Polsons came round to the apartment – this was in the first few months we were there when Dad was still alive – they got into a sort of discussion about religion and philosophy and so on with Mum and Dad.

"My parents were both religious but not in any conventional way...they didn't go to church but they believed in God. Anyway, they were talking about what the Polsons called the 'transmigration of souls'."

"What's that?" I asked.

"Well, I think it's about how the soul passes from one body into another at death."

"Like in reincarnation?" said Chrissie.

"I think so. But the thing I remembered was that Gerald Polson started talking about how souls can be made to transmigrate before death. It sounded really weird but he was saying how he and Monica, his wife, had been doing some kind of research – he made it sound very clinical and academic – that would prove conclusively that it could be achieved..."

We stared at her for a few moments in

silence. Then Col said, "You think that's what they may be doing with Jamie and Mark?"

"I know it sounds hard to believe–" Natalie said.

"I believe it," I broke in. It reminded me again of Hansel and Gretel and how the witch fed them every day so she could eat them. "I had this feeling, especially with Mark, of a soul in peril, but I still believe Mark's in there somewhere."

"So maybe Jamie – or Trancer – really *has* been sending out an SOS," Chrissie said.

We looked at her, mystified.

"SOS," she repeated. "Save Our Souls..."

Chapter 13

The days before we were to meet seemed to drag by endlessly. I was dying to ask mum if she had any knowledge or memory of the conversation I had with her in the safe room. But how could I explain seeing Jamie and Mark in the Polsons' house without both mum and dad putting their foot down and preventing me from returning the following Wednesday?

But it was mum who brought up the subject while we were eating dinner the following night. It was just her, me and Sophie as dad was working late.

As usual Sophie was grousing about how I was always allowed more freedom than her.

"And all I get is the blame," she grumbled. "Why can't I go to Nettie's with Abi next week?"

"Mum–" I protested.

"I think it's only fair, Abi," she said.

"But Nettie didn't invite Sophie, she only invited me."

I knew I was being mean, but at this stage it could ruin everything to have to bring her along. You may not believe this because I'm always putting her down, but I was genuinely worried about exposing her to all the risks we were about to take. I would never be able to forgive myself if something happened to her. But mum took the decision out of my hands.

"Actually, she has invited Sophie. I was

speaking to her today on the 'phone and she did say 'Please tell Sophie she's welcome to come too.' Besides, Abi, I know you'll take care of her. I think perhaps you're starting to understand the importance of letting into your life the thing that you're afraid of."

This was typical mum. She'd say something that could mean all sorts of things and leave it to you to decide how it applied to you.

"Thanks, Mum," Sophie said and poked her tongue at me.

"How do you mean?" I asked mum, ignoring this.

"Well, responsibility for a start. And then... well, perhaps you can think of some other examples?"

Suddenly the image flashed into my mind of Jamie's face as he recognised Trancer in my safe room.

"You don't mean–"

"Maybe we'll see Mark this time," Sophie said. "Maybe *he'll* be dancing in the window."

"Look after her if you go, Abi," mum said.

I sighed, wondering just how much mum really knew...

There was no alternative. If Sophie was going to be at Nettie's I had to let her in on what was going on and what we planned to do. But I had no intention of taking her with us to the Polsons' house.

"Why can't I come?" she protested.

It was typical of Sophie. Even though she had been spooked on our visit to the Polsons she now saw it all as a big, funny adventure which she didn't want to be left out of.

"'Cause you can't, and don't you dare mention this to Mum and Dad."

"What do you take me for?"

I had a million answers to that but for once I let her have the last word.

Lizzie came over the next day. She had broken up with her hippie.

"It didn't work out," she said glumly. "He had bad breath. And he wasn't even a hippie but a trainee estate agent in a blond wig."

I sympathised, but I was dying to tell her about Jamie and Mark.

"So you mean what I saw at the Phoenix was a ghost?" she said when I had finished.

"Well, like my mum says, there's more than one type of ghost. I believe that Trancer is a living part of Jamie. When Jamie travels out of his body he travels as Trancer."

"God, Abi, you're not going all strange and metaphysical on me, are you?"

"Come and see for yourself next Wednesday," I said.

She looked startled. "Really? I mean...well, I don't know..."

"Please, Lizzie, I need you there."

"To look after Sophie?"

I grinned. "How did you guess?"

At last Wednesday arrived. Tomorrow I would be back at school.

All my instincts and everything I had learnt so far about what the Polsons were doing to Jamie and Mark told me that this could be the last chance to rescue them before the Polsons' Trance Mission program enabled them not just to feed off the boys' psychic energy but to take over complete ownership of Jamie and Mark's souls.

Would we be in time or was it already too late?

Sophie, Lizzie and I travelled down from Swanleigh to London and at two o'clock we met up with Natalie, Chrissie and Col at Nettie's. We were all, in varying degrees, nervous and excited.

Nettie had left me the key and we waited in the living room with the lights off. We were too keyed up to talk, apart from Soph who kept asking if she could come with us, although we had already agreed that she was to stay at the flat with Lizzie and Chrissie. As three o'clock approached the tension became unbearable.

The minutes passed and still the car had failed to appear in the driveway. The garage door remained shut.

By twenty past three I was starting to think that we'd got the day wrong or that Nettie's information was unreliable. Could it be that I had left a tell-tale sign of my presence in the house and they had decided to vary their routine, or not leave the house at all? They could even have already departed, taking Jamie and Mark with them.

And then at last we saw the garage doors open and the car drive out. Sophie begged once again to come with Natalie, Col and me, and said how it wasn't fair, but Lizzie pulled out a computer game which she kept in her bag as a trump card for baby-sitting stroppy thirteen-year-olds and Soph became instantly engrossed in it.

Col had supplied us each with a walkie-talkie so we could keep contact with Chrissie and co. If we were not back by quarter to six, Lizzie and Chrissie would ring the police if contact was broken.

We took the same entrance route as before: I had warned Natalie and Col about getting through the nettles and climbing through the hole in the fence and they had kitted themselves up like commandos on a night raid.

In ten minutes we had penetrated the Polsons' driveway. Col was well-prepared. A friend of his who worked for a locksmith had supplied him with a set of skeleton keys, but getting into the kitchen from the utility room was the easy bit.

I had of course warned him about BBJ, so Col had got Chrissie to sneak two or three heavy sedative pills from their dad's surgery. He had ground these into a tinful of dog food which we'd brought with us in a plastic container.

"I know how to do this," he said, "because I used to help Dad in the surgery. I even wanted to be a vet myself, but then I caught the bug. Computers of course."

"The problem will be how long it takes for the sedative to take effect," he added. "It could be anything between twenty and thirty minutes. I'm going to put the bowl by the kitchen door. I hope I'll be able to handle him, but you'd better be prepared for me to make a quick exit."

Even from outside in the driveway where Natalie and I were waiting, we could hear BBJ going berserk as Col entered the utility room. After a minute his barking became even louder as Col opened the kitchen door with the skeleton key. The barking continued for a few seconds and then stopped and a moment later Col re-emerged in the driveway, looking slightly pale. He slammed the utility room door behind him.

"He's gone for it...but only just," he said when he'd caught his breath. "But I'm afraid it may take a while."

For the next twenty minutes we waited tensely in the driveway. For the first few minutes BBJ was obviously preoccupied with his meal, but then the barking started up again and the time seemed to stretch by interminably.

"How's it going?" came Lizzie's voice on the walkie-talkie.

"We're still waiting for BBJ to go to sleep,"

Col replied.

"Have you found Mark yet?" Sophie broke in.

I wished we'd saved one of the sedatives for her.

After ten or fifteen minutes BBJ seemed to calm down and five minutes later the barking stopped altogether.

Natalie and I were itching to go in, but Col stopped us.

"Give it another few minutes and he'll be out." He grinned. "My animal rights friends will probably never talk to me again but I'll just have to live with that."

When we finally entered the utility room we found BBJ lying unconscious in the middle of the floor.

"When do you think he'll wake up?" I asked anxiously.

"Couple of hours at the outside." He looked at his watch and I checked mine. It was gone four o'clock. "We'd better get moving."

Col went through to the study and sat down at the computer. We watched as he hacked through the security into the CD-ROM system and interfaced his own VR headset to connect to the programs which the master console was feeding through to Jamie and Mark.

"My God!" he exclaimed and almost threw off the headset. "I don't know what this stuff is, but it's doing my head in. It's lethal!"

I didn't care to see for myself and nor did Natalie. We left him to shut down the program and insert another disc, one that he had prepared with Natalie's help.

It was time to see Jamie and Mark...

I put a hand on Natalie's shoulder as we approached the cellar entrance. "Don't worry, Natalie," I whispered. "It'll be alright."

I had tried to prepare her for the shock but her face went a deadly white as she leaned towards the peephole and got her first view of her brothers for nearly five years. I could see her mouthing their names silently and when she lifted her face from the fisheye lens she was crying.

"How could anyone do that to another human being?" she sobbed. "How could they do that to Jamie and Marky? Why didn't I stop it?"

"Don't blame yourself, you weren't to know."

"But I did know. I felt they were evil and I did nothing!"

"You're here now, it's not too late," I said, with as much confidence as I could muster.

"I've switched the program," Col said from behind us and I relayed this information to Lizzie and Chrissie on the walkie-talkie.

Col peered into the viewer and when he looked up I could see that he was also badly shaken.

"They're like–"

"Zombies," I finished and he nodded.

"This has got to work," he muttered, but I could hear doubt in his voice.

We took turns to watch as the new VR program was fed to Jamie and Mark. Col had switched on a monitor which could be viewed directly from the peephole and which must have been switched off on my last visit, because I didn't remember seeing it. We were now able to see something of what was being relayed to the boys on their headsets.

Using advanced computer graphics Col had brought to life vivid and dynamic virtual reality scenes from their childhood, which Natalie had assembled from snapshots, mementoes, videos and the boys' favourite cassettes before the Canons left for Germany.

Natalie had dictated a voice-over to go with the other sounds and images on the disc and Col had made a copy on a small hand-held cassette recorder that we could listen to at the same time as it was being played back on their headsets. He switched it on.

"Hello, Jamie...hello, Mark...it's me...Natalie. It's been such a long time since I've seen you that, well, you may have thought I was dead or maybe you've forgotten me, but I've never forgotten you."

On the screen was a video of Natalie, talking to the camera, which Col had filmed a few days earlier.

The boys sat rigidly still. I had no idea if they could see or hear her.

"I've thought about you every day since I left Germany, but then that wasn't a good time and I don't think it's been a good time for you since we left home in London..."

The screen faded out and into a close-up of Jamie and Mark wearing paper hats as they sat with their family round the Christmas table. Jamie was leaning into the camera, crossing his eyes and pushing up his nostrils with his fingers, while Mark was half-collapsed under the table in hysterics...

"Do you remember, Jamie, Marky, when we were all a family together, remember all those Christmases and birthdays, the family picnics on the Surrey Downs and how we used to go tobogganing down the hill behind the school..."

The visuals changed, intercut with snapshots of the children, music from their childhood, pictures of their favourite toys and games.

The boys were like statues. I tried putting myself into their minds. To think like they thought...

I am in a computer program. I am the program. I don't know any difference between the program and myself. The program is my life, my God, my mother, my father, my food, my air, my thoughts, my sleep. I live because of it. Without it I do not exist...

The program has now been interrupted. I am in standby mode. I am waiting for my program to resume. I cannot respond to another program because I have not been programmed to do so...I am shut down, suspended until I am restarted...

Could it be like that? Could they be beyond the reach of any other programming, unable to even compute Col's video let alone respond to it? The thought was somehow more terrifying than the voice that had roared in my head on my previous visit; the voice that seemed to come from Mark...

"Do you remember Abi and Sophie who used to live across the road?" Natalie was saying, and suddenly there we were on the monitor, playing with the boys in their back garden. The video must have been taken during the summer before we left for Swanleigh, because we were all dancing to a song that was in the charts that year.

"They're here, Abi's here. And she wants to talk to you."

Suddenly I was there on camera, looking apprehensive as I began talking to the boys.

"Hello, Jamie and Mark, I hope you'll see this but I just don't know because I think sometimes you can't see or don't want to see... I just want to tell you, Jamie, that I know there's a part of you that's been trying to get through to me and that's why I saw you dancing in your window...and then I saw you again at the festivals, though you called yourself Trancer...and we got to be good friends until Trancer went away again. Anyway, the next time I saw you was here in the house and you didn't seem to know me again, but just at the end you did remember me, and I saw you dancing again at the window…

"This probably isn't making any sense but I believe you're both still in there, though you don't know it, and you don't have to live this way, plugged into machines all the time. You can be like you used to be in the old days when we used to go to school together…do you remember the hidey-hole we used to have, Jamie? When we buried the treasure?"

On the video I held up the silly striped purple knitted bobbly Rasta hat which Jamie had got his gran to knit for him one winter. He'd worn it almost continuously for two or three months after that, even though everyone used to make jokes about it, like calling him Noddy, and then he'd suddenly gone off it. So we'd decided to bury it, "to see if it could stand the test of time".

While my video had been playing, Col had dubbed techno music onto the sound and then I'd put the stripy hat on my head and started dancing, imitating Jamie's quirky movements, all flailing arms and wavy wrists.

"This is how you used to dance, Jamie. And you still dance like that…ask Trancer, Jamie… he knows how you dance."

It was at that moment that, on camera, I had started crying.

Natalie and Col, who had already seen the video, had let me watch through the fisheye lens of the peephole all this time, so I had an uninterrupted view, not just of the film on the monitor, but of Jamie and Mark.

Mark remained immobile, arrested, catatonic.

But in the last few seconds of the film I started to see a subtle change come over Jamie. Still locked into his headset his whole body began to writhe as though he were fighting some inner demon.

His movements became wilder, and he started thrashing around in his seat until he finally stood up and yanked off his headset, looking towards the staircase at the far end of the basement lab. I gasped with surprise and joy. His eyes were full of tears. He ran up the stairs and opened the door, falling into Natalie's arms and hugging her and then me.

But all the while this was going on I began to hear the voice again.

Just as it had the last time it came roaring into my head like a train coming out of a tunnel, and I could see from Natalie and Col's expressions that they could hear the voice too.

Down in the cellar Mark hadn't moved, but I knew without the shadow of a doubt that he was transmitting the voice.

Get out...we don't need you...you are not wanted...

And then there came a new and chilling message:

Trance mission...prepare to annihilate...

We looked at each other in horror. Was Mark still hooked into the previous program or was he now responding to Col's new program?

In that case we were all in imminent danger of being destroyed as Mark prepared to execute the figures of his early childhood, including himself.

Or was this part of what Natalie had told us about: was Polson about to complete the transmigration of Mark's soul and erase the boy's identity forever?

Or was he simply about to destroy anyone who stood in his way?

Chapter 14

I don't know if you've ever had a message in your head that you were about to be annihilated, but it can do funny things to you.

For a start your stomach turns to jelly and you start to realise what a wonderful job your knees normally do carrying the rest of your legs around, because now they seem quite incapable of doing the job at all and you have a strong urge to sit down.

And then you begin to appreciate how quietly and efficiently your heart goes about its business most of the time, without going on strike or making a nuisance of itself and acting like a hooligan, because now it's doing just that and you can't really do anything about it because you're having problems breathing.

And then it gets worse and you know you're starting to panic.

Well, I was, and I imagine everyone else was too, but we all seemed to be panicking so quietly that you wouldn't have known it.

There was only one person who could stop Mark now, I thought. Only one person who could communicate with him and possibly still even influence him.

We pleaded with Jamie to do something, but he was still dazed and confused, too upset to respond.

Trance mission...preparing to annihilate in

three minutes...

"Jamie, do something!" Natalie begged but Jamie still clung to us, like one of those soggy bits of greens you can't scrape off the plate.

In the lab, Mark hadn't moved but you could tell that he was concentrating all his psychic energy on the task he was programmed to perform.

How different the two boys were now. Where had all Jamie's brightness and energy gone?

This gave me an idea. I looked him in the eyes.

"Jamie, if you can't do it, let Trancer have a go."

He didn't seem to hear me. But then I saw the light come into his eyes and the flicker of a smile play on his lips.

"Maybe it's time we swapped a few dance steps."

"Jamie!"

For a second I thought he was asking me to dance, and even for Trancer this was taking coolness in the face of danger a little far. Then I remembered Reading.

It was what Trancer had said when I had told him about Jamie.

He suddenly looked shamefaced, but then said without a trace of irony, "I'm sorry, Abi, I didn't mean to sound flippant. I'll do my best..." Then he looked at me uncertainly. "By the way, who's Trancer?"

He squeezed my hand and Natalie's and returned down the lab steps to his console. He put on the headset and I could see he was focusing his mind on the same images as Mark.

"Do you think we should go down?" I asked Natalie.

"Yes," she replied. "They both need our support. We need to concentrate our minds on Mark and how much we love him."

As we descended into the lab, I could feel a crackly, fizzing, explosive electricity in the atmosphere and I knew this was coming from the clash of wills and psychic energy between the two brothers. It was as though their voices were fighting for control of the airwaves in my head.

Trance mission...preparing to annihilate in two minutes...

Remember me, Marky? Remember mum and dad and Natalie. She's come back. We all love you.

Preparing to annihilate...everything must be destroyed...

As the countdown reached ninety seconds, Col, who was standing beside me, started to panic.

"We're going to die and it's all my fault!" he shouted. "I set up this program and now it's going to kill us...I have to shut the computer down!"

He rushed upstairs to the study, but the countdown continued inside our heads and the battle intensified.

Trance mission...preparing to annihilate in one minute...

As the screens of the monitors went blank, Jamie jumped up from the console and ripped the headset off Mark's head. Mark turned on him, and there was a look on his face that I'll never forget – a blank, inhuman fury – and, without moving a finger, he sent his older brother flying back against the opposite wall of the lab.

At the same moment I heard a commotion in the hallway above and suddenly Sophie came crashing down the stairs, closely followed by Chrissie, Lizzie and Col.

As she took in the appalling scene – Mark standing like a robotic terminator, as though all he was at that moment was a supercharged brain, lasering bolts of high-voltage electricity at his older brother who was trying without much success to pull himself up from the floor – Sophie freaked.

"Marky," she screamed, bursting into tears, "what have they done to you?"

The countdown had reached twenty-five seconds when Mark faltered, staring at her.

I tried to stop her but Sophie shook me off and rushed over to Mark, holding her hands out to him. He stared at her hand. And then, reluctantly, as though he had been distracted from a purpose that was all he had existed for until a few seconds ago, but which had suddenly become pointless and irrelevant, he took it in his.

Trance mission...aborting...

The voice was now barely audible.

At eight seconds the countdown in our heads petered out.

I felt as though little Mark Canon, who I had last seen when he was six, had suddenly, seven years on, entered the room. And he had no idea what was happening or what he had been about to do.

He looked around at our faces, confused and bewildered – and then saw Jamie.

"What are you doing on the floor, you wally? Hi, Natalie, I'm really hungry. And I've got a terrible headache."

He stared at Sophie again. "Aren't you Sophie Edwards? What are *you* doing here?"

"They wouldn't let me come with them, Mark, to rescue you. But then the walkie-talkie went dead and–"

Mark looked at her in bewilderment. "Rescue me from what? Why are you all looking so strange? Like you've seen a ghost!"

That's when we all fell on him, hugging him, laughing and crying.

"I think we're the ghosts, Mark," Jamie said. "Someone did something very bad to us, but I can't remember much about it."

"That sounds like Trancer," I said.

He looked at me in astonishment. "You said something about Trancer before. For some reason it makes me think me of a dream I kept having...I think I was dancing..."

"You were, Jamie."

"But how do you know about it?"

I was about to answer him when I saw something out of the corner of my eye that made my skin crawl and my heart race.

In the hallway above I could hear BBJ barking again, the effects of the sedative clearly having worn off, but that wasn't what was scaring me.

Natalie had seen it too, for the blood drained from her face until it was white with fear.

"It's them!" she said, and I felt the anger that was welling up in her.

Everyone turned towards the cellar staircase.

I watched what appeared to be a pool of black ink that was slowly dropping from step to step – and then suddenly I knew what I was seeing.

The long shadow of Gerald Polson was slowly descending into the cellar...

Chapter 15

Instinctively, we retreated from Polson as he walked towards us.

His face was as black as thunder and he stared contemptuously at all of us, as though we were cockroaches who'd crawled through the chinks in the walls of his precious laboratory and who he would need to crush under his foot.

"James and Mark!" he said curtly, in that unctuous, creepy, smooth-as-velvet voice. "Return to your workstations: we will debrief later. Trance Mission stage three, version four, point six."

To my horror, I watched as his words seemed to operate just like the hypnotic trigger on a group of 'subjects' which I'd seen on a TV programme a few months earlier. Jamie and Mark instantly reverted to their trancelike state and sat down in their seats at the workstation, though the screens remained blank.

He smiled and turned back to the rest of us, instinctively homing in on Col.

"I notice you have attempted to delete several programs we are currently running, but we do of course back-up all our work on a continuous basis. Our research and preparations have taken many years, as I am sure you, Natalie, may possibly appreciate, and we will not allow it to be interrupted. The computer is of course on a network system and we are linked to other computers, other minds, in many parts of the world. We have important contacts. This cannot be stopped. Our work must go on. I repeat, our work must go on."

He pressed a switch on one of the computers and the screens came alive. I glanced at them and felt my head starting to pound again as the images and data began spewing out at a phenomenal speed.

"As for the rest of you," he went on, turning to face us, "in breaking into our house and interfering with our work, you have made a basic error in imagining that there could be any purpose in your being here.

"Goals and purposes are for those who have a role in the structure of life here on earth; most people have no such role but they are unfortunately still allowed to exist. They are of no concern to us.

"What is of concern to us is our research and experimentation, which will fundamentally change humanity. This work has now reached a crucial stage. Your complete ignorance of its importance does not exempt you from having to accept the consequences of your interference.

"You have no function because you have no future. You are, in a sense, already dead, but your actual death will allow us to monitor the progress of a particularly vital stage in our research, which is the annihilation process at the physical level by transmission of the appropriate instructions through our subjects here," he indicated Jamie and Mark.

"Their psychic energy levels are, at this very moment, being supercharged and the process should be completed in–" he looked at his watch, "–approximately four minutes."

"You mean you're getting my brothers to do your dirty work for you...to kill us," Natalie shouted angrily. "You're just scum...filthy, evil scum. You used my parents and destroyed them when you'd finished with them and you nearly destroyed Jamie and Mark–"

"Far from it, Natalie," Polson smiled. "Why should we wish to destroy what is useful to us? James and Mark are very much part of our future. When the transmigration process is complete we will have integrated their energies within ourselves."

"You *are* going to take over their souls," I gasped.

Polson turned to me and once again I felt myself going weak under that horrible mesmerising gaze.

"Souls...what a small, imperfect word, and quite inadequate as a formula for defining and quantifying the whole range of electrical energies which make up the inner potential of a human being. But yes...Abigail, you do seem fond of coming here, don't you...you are correct. We already have complete access to our subjects' electrical blueprints and their transference to ourselves is of paramount importance. What, in comparison, is the value of so-called souls to these subjects?"

"They're not subjects," Sophie broke in angrily, "they're Jamie and Mark!"

Polson ignored her. "Of themselves, James and Mark are nothing, any more than any of you are. But they are extremely effective tools, as I am about to demonstrate. Unfortunately, none of you will live to appreciate the results."

Without even turning, he fired out another order.

"Trance Mission stage four!"

So this was it, I thought, we're all going to die.

I should have been paralysed with fear, but I wasn't. Why was that? What was it that was different about the atmosphere since Jamie and Mark had seemed to switch back into their state of trance?

Of course!

It was the voice.

The voice that Mark had sent spinning through my brain, making it hard for me to think. The voice that had terrified me so much it had caused me to open the door into my safe room to seek a refuge from it.

I couldn't hear it.

If Jamie and Mark were concentrating their psychic energy on some target with a view to annihilation, that target wasn't me, and looking round at Sophie and co, I somehow knew that they couldn't hear the voice either.

I glanced towards Jamie and Mark in time to see a look darting between them, a kind of psychic nod of agreement.

The next moment the cellar floor began to shake and I started to feel rather than hear a deep, reverberating sound, like the rumbling engines of a ship or the start of an earthquake.

The reverberations increased until every molecule in my body seemed to be churning in rhythm with the vibrations. The last thing I remember before I blacked out was seeing Lizzie, Chrissie and Sophie clinging to each other for dear life; Jamie and Mark were standing up, looking at me but somehow beyond me, and then the lights went out, plunging the cellar into darkness as the lab machinery began to explode...

When I came to, I could hardly believe what I was seeing.

The lab was on fire, the computer equipment had disintegrated; some bits of machinery were still burning, sending out an acrid smoke that made me cough and splutter; others, like the VDUs, had simply imploded.

But it was as if Sophie, Natalie, Chrissie, Lizzie, Col and I were in a fireproof zone, as though an invisible shield were protecting us.

As for Jamie and Mark, they were standing exactly as I had last seen them, except that they were now looking upwards towards the ceiling.

Where to my astonishment I saw Polson suspended like a chandelier.

As I watched him he slowly started to spin

and then they seemed to be revving up their psychic engine because he spun at increasing speed until he suddenly crashed to the floor.

Even now there was something about him that frightened me; as though he could still reach into himself and find a button that would allow him to recover every bit of the control he'd exerted over the boys for the past few years.

But as he picked himself up, his eyes bulging with rage and the veins swollen in his forehead, there was a noise at the top of the stairs that made everyone turn.

Standing there in black twinset and pearls, looking as though she had been waiting all her life for this moment, Mrs Munster reminded me of the old silent film actress in *Sunset Boulevard* who has gone completely mad and thinks she is a star once again.

It would have been hilarious, except that she had a revolver in her hand.

"Shoot them, now!" Polson shouted, the oiliness in his voice obliterated by coarse, venomous, choking rage.

She pointed the gun somewhere between Natalie, Col and me.

"Not them! They're sewage! We'll flush them away later. Shoot the boys!"

Monica Polson faltered. "But Gerald, we can't kill them, not at this stage...we need them. We'd have to start all over again–"

"Kill them!" Polson screamed. "They're rabid. Shoot them like dogs!"

Reluctantly she pointed the revolver at Jamie and Mark, but there was something that seemed to be stopping her from pulling the trigger.

"What's the matter with you?" Polson stormed. "Didn't you hear me? Shoot them!"

Jamie and Mark seemed to be completely unperturbed and I realised that they were still looking ahead at nothing in particular.

But then slowly, acting in unison, as though connected by a common brain, they turned towards Mrs Munster.

The revolver trembled in her hand and then, slowly, she turned her body and pointed it at her husband.

"No–" he screamed and then she shot him three times, once in the head and twice in the heart.

Then, almost mechanically, she turned the gun on herself, pressed the barrel to her temple and pulled the trigger.

Chapter 16

The police had finished their questioning for the day. Mum and dad had arrived and so had Lizzie's mum and Chrissie and Col's parents.

We were all back in Duncan and Nettie's living room, even BBJ who, in Mr Somers' expert hands, had rolled over on his back with his paws in the air.

So Big Bad Jonah wasn't really so bad after all.

We were all very tired but deliciously happy, especially Mark and Jamie.

"I'm starting to remember the dreams," Jamie said, as we sat together a little apart from the others. "I used to find myself dancing in all kinds of strange places. I once even danced with a group of Aborigines on a beach somewhere in Australia..."

"Perhaps you were in dream time," I said. "That's what the Aborigines believe in, that there's another reality, a kind of parallel universe, where we all live, but we don't know it because we only go there in our dreams."

"I must have gone there when I saw you," Jamie said. "I remember how when you touched my face, I felt as though someone was trying to wake me up... But if I was in dream time and you were in real time, how did we meet?"

"Maybe there are crossover places between the two universes, and that's how you could send me messages. But how could you have lived like that, hooked up to those machines for all that time?"

"I can't tell you much about it, because I don't remember now, but I expect I will in time ...that's what I'm afraid of."

"It may come back to you in dreams," I said.

"If it does, I'll call out to you to rescue me again."

"But will you appear as yourself or as Trancer?"

"Who's Trancer?"

I stared at him. "Don't tell me you've forgotten again."

Jamie grinned. "Only kidding. Once you mentioned it to me it all started to come back to me. I know that's what I called myself when we met at that festival. And then I remember meeting him in this room, but it was like when you used to live here."

"You remember that?" I said in astonishment. "But that only happened in my mind. I introduced you to Trancer in my mind, in my safe room – I created a little room in my mind where everything would be safe, when I was frightened by the voice Mark transmitted into my head."

He looked puzzled. "This voice...what sort of things did it say?"

"It said things like 'Get out, we don't need you...'"

"I remember that voice...it didn't really come from Mark, though it sounded like him, it came from the Polsons. They put all those programs into our heads. It was like we were being brainbathed–"

"Brainwashed," I corrected him.

"Okay, so I've forgotten a few words. I've been out of circulation for five years, remember, except that I was able to escape sometimes."

"Into *your* safe room?"

"Yes," he said, "I always felt safe when I was dancing. But it never seemed to last."

"You mean when you'd start to turn into a zombie?"

"Who's calling who a zombie?"

"Me. I just called you a zombie."

"You mean I was like this?" He crossed his eyes and turned instantly into the undead and I broke up laughing.

Nettie, observing him, whispered to mum, "Poor kids, it'll take years to undo the mental damage. And a lot of counselling. Do you know any good counsellors?"

"I know a couple who won't be available," Natalie said drily.

"I think after what they've been through, what they need is a good home with a lot of love and plenty of decent food and rest," mum said. "What do you think, Paul?"

Dad gave her a searching look. "Are you thinking what I think you're thinking?"

"I didn't know you could be so telepathic," she smiled.

"In that case, as long as you promise there'll

be no psychic tests–"

"And no computers," mum added.

"Then maybe Jamie and Mark could come and live with us," dad said. "Of course, we'll have to get through all the red tape, but that shouldn't be a problem. What do you think, kids?"

We stared at each other open-mouthed.

"Can Mark sleep in my room?" Sophie said excitedly.

Mum and dad exchanged glances.

"I don't think that's a good idea, Soph," mum said diplomatically. "For the time being you and Abi can share a room until we can sort out the best sleeping arrangements."

"Mum!" we both protested, but then we both decided you couldn't have everything.

"It's time we did some home improvements anyway, Paul," mum said. "What about converting the spare room into two more bedrooms?"

"Mmmm," said dad. "I might need a bit of help though."

"You'd better not count on Duncan," Nettie muttered, and we all laughed, except Duncan.

"Really, Net, that's not fair. If you knew how much time I was spending–"

"...on the Eurostar," Nettie completed wearily. "Yes, I've heard you mention it a couple of times."

"What's Swanleigh like?" Jamie asked.

"Don't raise your hopes too high," I warned him. "Let's just say, I am the only significant cultural icon in a village boasting thirty-odd houses, a pub and a single shop that doesn't even sell foaming beauty wash."

Sophie meanwhile was becoming re-acquainted with Mark.

"Do you like Take That?" she asked him.

"What's that, a card game?"

Sophie rolled her eyes.

"You've got a lot to catch up on."

Epilogue

So that's how Jamie and Mark came to live with us. In the end dad did convert the spare room with help from Duncan who was a reformed character after Nettie had insisted he worked on the baby's nursery which used to be my bedroom and where I had first seen Jamie dancing in the window.

Duncan and Nettie had their baby, whom they called Katie, and whenever I visit them I take her to the park in her pram, but I keep away from the alleyways because the house they lead to is now a bad house.

It has been bought and sold twice – "They left pretty sharp because of the weird vibes," Nettie told me – and has now been left vacant and ramshackled, its windows blacker than ever, and I've always tried to avoid even looking at it.

But one afternoon in Katie's room I couldn't help glancing out of the window, and for a split second I thought I saw a flash of orange at the window.

As mum says, there's more than one type of ghost, but it couldn't have been Jamie because he and Mark are now back at school, both making good progress, though Jamie was miffed when he was put in the same class as Mark...and I don't blame him.

The thought of having to be in the same

class as Sophie makes my hair stand on end, and to tell you the truth, it's as scary to me as anything that happened to us that summer.

Jamie and Mark are more or less back to their old selves, and as the adoption went through without a hitch we now have two brothers, so you can imagine how noisy mealtimes are.

"Sometimes I think I'm invisible round here," Sophie complains.

"Who said that?" Jamie and I say together, looking round the room in mock terror and Mark collapses in giggles.

But sometimes, late at night, Jamie wakes up screaming, then me or mum will go into his bedroom and put our arms round him and tell him it's a nightmare and he's safe now.

Strangely enough, Mark seems to have forgotten the whole experience. But I know that something inside him hasn't, because of what happened last week.

I dreamt I was back at the house across the road, frozen in terror between Big Bad Jonah and Jamie and Mark who stood across the hallway, and as the dog's barking increased, the voice came roaring once again into my head.

"Please stop it!" I begged them. "It's over... Jamie...Mark, it's over, isn't it?"

And then Jamie turned into Trancer and began dancing in front of me.

But Mark remained immobile, implacable, unseeing, and the voice grew in volume until it was unbearable...

I woke up and rushed to Jamie's room, but he met me on the landing.

"I've been having an awful dream," he said.

And without speaking we knew it was the same dream.

We went into Mark's room to check that he was okay.

He was sitting up in bed, rigid.

His eyes were open and he was back in the trance.

Next morning he seemed to have no memory of the incident. "Come along, you lot," dad said, "I'll run you to school."

"Do we *have* to go to school today?" said Sophie.

"I like school," said Jamie. "What about you, Mark?"

Mark looked up and there was a glint in his eyes that I thought looked new and different but somehow familiar, although I couldn't say from where.

"The work must go on," he said.